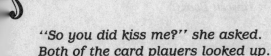

"So you did kiss me?" she asked.

Both of the card players looked up.

He smiled blandly over at his mother, who blinked slowly and then returned to her game. "Please keep your voice down, Miss Mills," he said, still smiling for the benefit of the others. In the same low tones he continued, "I know it was incorrect of me. I assure you it will never happen again."

"If it does, I shall be sober so that I may decide if I want to kiss you."

The statement shocked him into silence. At length he intoned, "Miss Mills, the situation will not arise again."

"You must have wanted to kiss me. I had drunk too much wine, but you had not."

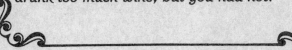

Also by Rebecca Ashley
Published by Fawcett Books:

THE RIGHT SUITOR
A LADY'S LAMENT
A SUITABLE ARRANGEMENT
LADY FAIR
FEUDS AND FANTASIES
RUINS AND ROMANCE

AN AWKWARD ARRANGEMENT

Rebecca Ashley

FAWCETT CREST • NEW YORK

To Eva, with gratitude and affection

A Fawcett Crest Book
Published by Ballantine Books
Copyright © 1992 by Lois Walker

Library of Congress Catalog Card Number: 92-90611

ISBN 0-449-22087-7

Manufactured in the United States of America

First Edition: October 1992

Chapter 1

"IT IS only a temporary problem, Lawrence," Henry said earnestly. "Do not refine too much on this."

Lawrence gazed around the half-empty room and then speechlessly back at his younger brother. Lawrence did not care that his many-caped riding coat dripped onto the gleaming stone floor in a trail of glistening drops or even that he was tired from his long drive up from London. He had ordered his carriage brought round immediately after receiving Henry's ominous message. Now Lawrence was too stunned to think about comfort.

"I have no doubt I can recover the silver plate within a fortnight or so." Henry sighed before continuing, "I fear the gold wall sconces will have been melted down. But the furniture cannot be melted," he added in an attempt at cheerfulness. "We can surely find the chairs and tables." He gave a bracing smile, displaying the even row of teeth and the twinkling gray eyes that had resulted in a dozen debutantes falling hopelessly in love.

Lawrence, taller and older than his brother, was possessed of the same fine gray eyes beneath heavy black brows. He had the family's Roman nose, strongly etched cheekbones, and a fine male frame.

1

He was also capable of smiling, although sometimes in a slightly mocking manner.

He was not smiling now. Nor was the earl of a mood to appreciate Henry's winsome smile. Lawrence's thoughts toward his brother grew even darker as he surveyed the room again. The entrance to Wicklowe Hall had originally been built as part of a monastery. The central hall where the monks had taken their bread had been preserved to form the entrance hall in the fifteenth century when the Wicklowes began building their home. That was shortly after old Robert Eldridge was made the first earl following "distinctive service." This had taken the form of providing a handsome loan to the king. Whether the loan had been to King Henry IV or V or VI had been muddied in the waters of family history.

"Henry," Lawrence said in measured tones, "let me be certain I understand. You gave the house over to a gypsy to manage. He and the rest of his band stole the fittings from the rooms and half the furniture, and now he is gone." If he sounded incredulous, it was no less than how he felt. Henry was young and foolish, but this was beyond anything Lawrence could have imagined.

Henry squared shoulders almost as large as the earl's and said, "He was not precisely a gypsy, Lawrence. He was of noble birth on his mother's side, although she was shunned by her family after the marriage. I would not call him a gypsy. He was a bit olive of skin, yes, and he did know the gypsies encamped on the hillside nearby, but he seemed trustworthy. I had several excellent conversations with him over at the alehouse. As I said, he was of superior birth along his mother's side."

2

"I do not care about the particulars of the black-guard's birth," Lawrence snapped. "I want to know where the devil he is now." Thank heavens Mother was visiting her sister in Kent and was not here to see the empty house or she would have succumbed to hysteria. More important than even Mother, however, was getting everything back in order before September. That was when the Prince Regent himself was coming to Wicklowe Hall. Lawrence was determined that everything be perfection when he arrived.

Henry looked mournfully down at the tips of his Hessian boots. "There's the rub. No one knows where he has gone. He was here not four days ago. It appears one of the housemaids departed with him, and I fear she took some of the finer linens with her."

Bother the linens. The important things were the priceless pieces of furniture. "Are the gypsies that were encamped on the hillside also gone?"

"Yes."

Lawrence bit back his groan. He would have sunk onto the Louis XIV chair, a gift from King George I to their great-grandfather, had the chair been where it had always stood. There was a vacant place along the wall where it should have been. Even the richly hued Aubusson carpet with its swirls of blue and red and gold was gone, leaving the stone floor bare. Lawrence could only surmise the rug had left the house on the gypsy's back. He didn't doubt the man had had plenty of help carrying things out.

"Where were the footmen and maids while our property was being stolen?" the earl demanded.

Henry's chin sunk low against the folds of his cravat. He looked like a puppy fearing a heavy

3

scolding. "They were given a party that evening and offered all the stout they cared to drink. Apparently many of them cared to imbibe a great deal. They were so merrily drunk, some even helped load the furniture."

Seeing the murderous rage rising up on his brother's face, Henry said quickly, "I know you have been traveling and are tired to death." He tried another smile. "I disliked troubling you, but Prinny is coming, and I thought you would want to know about the house."

Lawrence was indeed tired, but he had far too many questions he wanted answered. "Why did you leave this man in charge?"

"I told you, Lawrence." Henry managed to convey a wounded expression while he stood in the center of the empty room and tugged at the gold links of his watch fob. "I had to be gone a short time, and Stinson was ill. I could scarcely go away and leave the house without anyone in charge. That would have been irresponsible, and you know you are always impressing on me the need to be mindful of my position and of the family name."

Lawrence stared at his younger brother. "Placing a stranger in charge of one's property does not precisely fulfill the need to be responsible, especially when the stranger is a thief you met in an alehouse."

"I said I was sorry."

Henry looked as cowed and anxious as Lawrence had ever seen him, but that only diminished his anger a little. Yet he realized he was wasting time making accusations. At the moment, the important thing was to find a solution. Once the furniture was safely returned, he could ring a peal over the young idiot's head. "What do you know about this gypsy?" That might help determine where the man was now and set the wheels in motion to recover their possessions.

Henry looked up from fidgeting with the watch fob, clearly relieved that there would be no more recriminations. Relaxing, he brushed his fingernails against the superfine of his blue coat and lounged back against the smoothly polished granite wall. "He brought a letter of acquaintance from Roger Blakely. You remember Roger, don't you? A bruising rider. A member of the Four-in-Hand Club and bang up to the mark in every way and—"

Lawrence interrupted impatiently, "Have you written to Roger Blakely to find out what he can tell us?"

Henry sighed. "Yes. Roger does not know William Jersey at all. Truth to tell, I doubt William Jersey is even his name. I thought it sounded very English for one so dark."

"A belated burst of insight," the earl muttered.

"It is not so bad as all that," Henry continued hastily. "Mother will be overset, but she will recover. It is past time we had a few new pieces of furniture in this old pile. That dining room table was well over two hundred years old. It is not a question of being able to afford new things since there's plenty of blunt in the family coffers. As to Prinny's visit, we might be able to borrow some furniture while he is here."

The earl drew himself up to his full height. "The treasures of Wicklowe House had been acquired through generations." Lawrence's words snapped like dry twigs. "They are valuable not only for their worth but because they are family heirlooms. As

5

the Earl of Wicklowe, I have an obligation to the future generations of this family, and I take my obligations seriously. We shall not borrow one stick of furniture for the Prince Regent's visit. We shall recover what is ours if it kills both of us." Frustrated and angry, he gave his riding crop a sharp snap.

Henry stopped buffing his nails and drew hastily upright. "What are we to do now?"

"Find this damned gypsy. It is plain as a pikestaff he will try to sell what he has stolen. There can only be a market for such treasures in a few places. London is the most obvious. We can start there."

Henry looked relieved. "I knew you would know what to do." He paused before asking carefully, "Would you object to retrieving the property yourself? I had hoped to ride with Sefton and Barrymore and Colonel Berkeley to the Windmill at Salt Hill when they go next week. Sefton has those superb bays, you know. My team will not look so splendid, but if they are willing to let me accompany them, perhaps I can buy some new bits of blood. Or borrow your excellent pair of grays," he suggested hopefully.

Lawrence leveled a quelling look. "If you think I mean to recover the stolen property myself so you can go off riding with this ridiculous group of men who have nothing better to do than play coachman, you will catch cold. You are going to be right beside me wherever I go." He fixed a steely eye on his brother and did not look away until Henry nodded his acquiescence.

"As you wish."

Lawrence's fondness for his younger brother tempered his anger. Lawrence had done some foolish things himself when he was one-and-twenty, although nothing as shatterbrained as this. In a quieter voice, he explained, "The Prince of Wales is coming to Wicklowe Hall to consult with me over architectural plans. I have not finished drawing the plans, so I am taking valuable time away from my work."

Lawrence was a gifted architect. Naturally he did not pursue it as a living, because it would have been beneath his station to work for money. He was honored, however, to be included in the select group the prince was gathering together to lay plans for a new London. He would be in the company of such a luminary as John Nash. Lawrence must have something impressive to show the prince when he arrived.

"The Four-in-Hand Club does not signify." Henry's words were without conviction, and he looked morose. "I daresay I can convince them to let me go with them later."

"Of course you can. Now then, we must begin by making a list of what is missing."

"I shall get paper and pen."

"You are going to be very pleased at the exquisite furnishings I have come into possession of. Very pleased, indeed." Mrs. Wiley's wide smile showed a gap between her middle teeth. She wore a bright red gown that would have been better suited for evening wear or for a masquerade ball. Her curls were an unusual shade of yellow. Molly did not believe Mrs. Wiley had come by the color naturally.

Molly and her thirteen-year-old cousin Antonia stood in the hallway and waited. The house smelled of mustiness and oil and cooked onions. Molly did

7

not object to the smell, but she was anxious to continue their business.

She tried to hurry things along. "I am eager to see what you have."

"In a moment," Mrs. Wiley said cheerfully, and toyed with the frill on the neckline of the red dress. "It would not be right to show you the treasures until you know their history. They have come from the palaces of kings." She threw one hand out in a grand theatrical gesture. "Kings!"

A servant had told Molly that Mrs. Wiley had trod the boards as an actress several years ago. That was before the older woman returned to Bath and undertook the business of buying and selling what Mrs. Wiley referred to as "distinguished remains of distinguished estates." That meant she trafficked in the sale of the household goods of impoverished barons or in the silver of earls who had gamed too foolishly and found themselves at point non plus.

"Kings?" Antonia's interest was piqued. Antonia was small for her age, fair-skinned, and possessed of the same red hair as Molly. Freckles dotted the bridge of her turned-up nose. She had a way of tilting her head to the side when she talked. "What kings?"

"It might have been George I. It very likely was, since one of the pieces is a fine example of silver gilt from that time period."

Molly plucked a long red hair from the shoulder of her dark cape and waited. She was not normally a patient person, but she was willing to wait because Mrs. Wiley had furniture to sell, and they were sorely in need of furniture. After all, there was all of Kindred Manor to equip.

Uncle Brace had purchased the house in England after his home in Ireland burned down six months ago. He had taken the fire as a sign it was time for him to return to England. He had persuaded Molly to come with them "just until Antonia and I are settled" and to help him fill the empty house he had purchased.

"I sent word to you before anyone else," Mrs. Wiley confided. "I know you are trying to furnish your house for your dear uncle. Naturally I wish to help in any way I can. I knew your uncle when he was a boy. That was before he went to Ireland. I was surprised when he returned." She paused, clearly waiting for Molly to say something. "Very surprised," she said pointedly.

Molly did not know why her uncle's return should surprise anyone. There was nothing exceptional about a man who had lived abroad returning to his home country. The English, however, were liable to think anything. Molly had been reared in Ireland in a genteel school for ladies. Her parents were of that rare breed of Irish who owned land and had money. She was dreadfully fond of Uncle Brace, and he was English, so she had thought the English could not be all bad even though the general feeling in Ireland was not favorable toward the English. Since coming to Bath, however, she was changing her mind.

People here had trouble understanding her even though she spoke perfectly correctly. Or else they thought she was quaint. "Say that again, dear, with that pretty little lilt," a woman in a shop on Milsom Street had coaxed the other day. To Molly, it was the English who spoke in hard, unpoetic words.

9

They talked through their noses without any music in their voices.

Mrs. Wiley sighed, clearly disappointed that neither Molly nor Antonia had taken the opportunity to enlighten her about why Sir Brace had returned. "I daresay you want to see what I have to sell. It is just behind this door." She pushed the stout oaken door open with a flourish.

Molly stepped inside and blinked. She had assumed Mrs. Wiley was exaggerating. Now, to her pleasure, Molly realized she was not. The room was stacked floor to ceiling with furniture. Even at a casual glance, she noted that the carvings on the nearby claw-foot table were exquisite. An armoire was made from unblemished, beautifully polished pine. Chairs were nested together. A handsome desk butted against a long dining table. A settee lay on its side. A bronze lampstand peeked from behind a *secrétaire*. Stacked high along the mantel and tilting at precarious angles were gleaming silver tureens and gilt-laden trays. The room contained a veritable treasure trove.

"This is wonderful," Molly breathed.

Even Antonia, who usually cared only for ancient illuminated manuscripts or for stories of ghosts in mist-shrouded castles, looked about with interest.

Mrs. Wiley beamed. "Did I not tell you? The settee is very fine. I recommend that you purchase it. And the sideboard. The plate and silver are also splendid. You really must look at everything closer."

Mrs. Wiley edged into the room, lifted her red skirts to step over a footstool, then turned to face her two customers. "I know it will take time to go through everything and decide what you want. I would not *think* of hurrying you. However, I must tell you someone else is coming within the hour who is also interested." She stopped and cocked her head, listening. "I shouldn't be surprised if that were his carriage I hear outside now. But do take your time in deciding what you want," she concluded with a dazzling smile.

Molly thought of the empty rooms of Kindred Manor. Outside she heard the carriage door shut. She had no need to examine each piece. "We shall take everything."

"All of it?" Mrs. Wiley's voice went shrill with delight.

Molly nodded firmly. "All of it."

"We have not spoken of price," Mrs. Wiley said delicately.

A knock sounded on the door.

"I am sure you will name a fair price." Money was not of great concern. Uncle Brace was rich and would be happy to buy such beautiful pieces. Now Molly could return to walking her Irish wolfhound, practicing calligraphy with Antonia, and preparing to return to Ireland.

Once Uncle Brace was settled comfortably, there would be nothing to hold Molly in England. She was eager to return to Ireland to see her family and Daniel Ryan. Unless she was badly mistaken, he had had marriage in his eyes when she boarded the boat to leave for England.

After an unsuccessful trip to London tramping about from purveyors of antiques to auction houses, Lord Lindworth and Henry arrived at Welton's. There, kindly and knowledgeable Mr. Welton had suggested they repair to Bath and seek out a certain Mrs. Wiley. She was known—here Mr. Welton had stopped to clear his throat delicately—for accepting property without thoroughly ascertaining its origin.

Three days later, Lawrence and Henry approached Bath. Their traveling carriage was excessively well sprung, and the tight windows kept out much of the road dust. Still, both brothers were powdered with a light coating of fine grit, and Lawrence was stiff from sitting so long. As he shifted about in search of a more comfortable position, he glowered at Henry. He was angry at his younger brother for being so foolish, angry at the gypsy for being a thief, and angry at himself for losing so much precious time when he ought to be working on architectural plans.

He could not even temper his ill humor with the thought he would have the opportunity to study the fine architecture of the city of Bath. The classically inspired buildings of John Wood, both elder and younger, included the Mineral Springs Hospital and King's Circus and were models of excellence, but he would not have time to enjoy these treasures. His time would be spent searching for his lost property. He ought to be in his St. James's Square home in London right now sketching his own plans.

The Prince Regent was bringing the eminent architect John Nash to Wicklowe Hall to discuss ways to fashion a more elegant and modern London, and Lawrence had promised to have sketches to show him. One might break a promise to a friend, but one did not break a promise to the future king of England. Besides, Lawrence's pride was at stake here. He knew he was a good architect, and he wanted some of his ideas implemented into buildings that would remain standing for years, even decades from now, as a tribute to his talent.

"We have not discussed where to stay," Henry roused himself to say. He had been slumped in the corner ruing the fact Lawrence had refused to spend last night at the Fin and Feather, where Henry's eye had settled on a certain innkeeper's daughter. Her name was Betsy, and she had been possessed of a neatly turned ankle and a saucy smile. He had mentioned her name several times today.

"I am sure the man at Welton's was wrong in sending us to Bath," Henry declared. "No one of any consequence will be there. Everyone is in London or Brighton save for a few bacon-faced squires and their wives. There will not even be a decent place to stay."

"We can take quarters at Laura Place or Camden Place."

Henry shifted grumpily. "Full of cheeseparing merchants and nabobs. I'd as lief sleep in the stables with the horses."

"Suit yourself, if the straw does not bother you. I intend to stay at Willow House." Henry was right, of course. No one except a few dowagers ever came to Bath to ride about in salon chairs, take the waters at Queen's Bath, and drink the foul-tasting water for its curative powers. Even the assembly rooms were dull. The sooner he and Henry completed their visit and left, the happier Lawrence would be.

Henry opened the window, and Lawrence looked out onto a hilly, curving valley. In the distance, the Avon rolled peacefully through the green valley, like a ribbon of blue silk. Brown cattle grazed in the fields.

It was an idyllic scene, Lawrence reflected, but it still did not compare with the majestic land surrounding Wicklowe Hall.

A few minutes later they reached the town and drove past the Royal Crescent, a curve of identical houses with immense ground floors and columns that soared twenty feet high.

"Shall we see to rooms first?" Henry asked.

Taking rooms and resting from the journey would be the sensible thing to do, Lawrence knew, but he was impatient to find Mrs. Wiley and get the matter sorted out. "I would rather conduct our business first."

"As you wish," Henry grunted.

Lawrence lifted one dark eyebrow at his brother, a silent reminder they were here because of Henry's foolishness.

"You are right to see to business," his younger brother added in hasty, apologetic tones.

The man at Welton's had provided them with directions to Mrs. Wiley's house, and Lawrence gave those to the driver. They proceeded down High Street, past a meadow, and into a less prosperous-looking area of shops. Finally they reached a tight little row of houses that hugged one another like lost children. The tall, straight houses were not precisely crumbling, but they had clearly endured better times.

Lawrence's black, crested carriage halted in front of a house where paint peeled in long white strips. A shutter was slanted away from the window, held to the building with nothing but a nail.

Henry looked dubiously out the window. "Can this be the right address? I cannot conceive that anything from Wicklowe Hall would end up *here*."

14

"We shall soon see." Lawrence alighted. His Hessians struck the cobbled walk briskly as he walked up to the door and knocked with the silver head of his walking stick.

The door was answered by a slight, nervous-looking maid.

"I wish to see Mrs. Wiley," he said in his most sonorous tones.

She looked at his riding coat, his fashionable trousers, and then behind him to the crested equipage and matching horses. She gasped and dashed away to search for her mistress.

The woman who appeared in the door a few moments later was tall, thin, and possessed of a head of improbable-looking blond hair. She was dressed in a gown festooned with acres of gold embroidery. The embroidery, he noted, was beginning to fray. She must have been above fifty, although she smiled flirtatiously at him and batted her eyes about. Lawrence introduced himself, presented his card, and waited.

Mrs. Wiley read the card. Her eyes widened, she clapped a hand to her breast, and she dropped a curtsy so deep, it nearly toppled her. The earl was obliged to put out a hand to steady her. She stumbled back to her feet and smiled at him, then at someone behind him.

Lawrence glanced over his shoulder and saw Henry standing beside the carriage. His brother watched warily as half a dozen surly-looking men gathered to inspect the magnificent carriage and sweat-dampened horses.

"Who is that?" she asked.

"My brother," he said shortly.

"Well, you must both come in and have tea. I have just this minute brewed a new pot."

15

"Thank you, Mrs. Wiley, but I must decline. We are here on a business matter of some importance. We are looking for a large shipment of furniture and plate. Some of it dates from the period of George the First."

"Furniture from the time of George the First?" She mulled that over as if she had never heard of that particular king.

"There would have been several very nice tables," Henry supplied helpfully from the street. "And some Adams chairs. Cherry, I think. Might have been walnut." He was distracted by an urchin trying to pull the ears of the lead horse. "Off with you, boy, or I'll pull *your* ears off."

Lord Lindworth waited for Mrs. Wiley's reply.

That good woman glanced from one to the other of her noble visitors. The earl could almost see her calculating the cost of his perfectly starched cravat, Weston-stitched blue coat, and trousers of mustard twill. "Now that I reflect, I did have a few such pieces, but they are sold."

"Sold, did you say?" Henry shouted. "Close that door and get away right now, you little wretch."

"Sold to whom?" Lawrence asked.

"To Sir Brace. Well, to his niece. Lovely gel she is, too. All red curls and flashing green eyes and such a pretty Irish way of speaking. She paid a handsome price." The older woman studied the elegant carriage, and her eyes narrowed in further calculation. "I expect you could buy everything back. I shall, of course, be glad to make inquiries and the necessary arrangements for only a modest sum."

The earl fixed her with a sharp stare. If she thought she was going to make additional money from him, she was fair and far out. "I have no intention of paying one sou to get my property back."

Mrs. Wiley blinked. "Your property?"

"Yes, it was stolen from us by the gypsy you must have purchased it from."

She started. "William Jersey is no gypsy, and he is certainly not a thief. He had a letter of introduction from Sir Roger Blakely himself."

"He must hire a scribe to draw letters up by the dozen," the earl muttered.

"What?"

"That gypsy does not know Sir Roger Blakely."

Mrs. Wiley started to argue further, but Lawrence forestalled her by asking, "Can you give me the direction of the woman who has my property?"

She surveyed the earl and his carriage one final time, then she threw a hand dramatically up to her forehead. "I am devastated to learn that I may have bought something which was come by dishonestly. I am quite, quite inconsolable."

"Where did you say this woman resides?"

She told him.

Lawrence thanked her, turned, and went down the steps. A large, dour-looking man with hands the size of wood axes was examining the carriage. Henry looked anxious but did not object, no doubt owing to the size of the man.

"Are we ready to leave?" Henry asked hopefully.

"Yes." Ignoring the large man, Lawrence gave directions to the driver and got inside. Once they were moving, he gave Henry a terse summary of the conversation. "It only remains for us to find this redheaded chit. Of course, she knew perfectly well that everything was stolen. Anyone with wits about her would question how such valuable pieces came to be in the possession of a person like Mrs. Wiley."

"Do you mean to go see this woman now?"

"No." Lawrence leaned back against the satin squabs. "I am tired. We shall hire rooms and send a note to her that we shall call tomorrow."

Tomorrow everything would be taken care of. Lawrence would have his treasured family possessions back, and he could return to London, and from there to Wicklowe Hall. Then he could direct his attention to his true interest, working on designs for a new London. It only remained for him to deal with this troublesome woman.

"Uncle Brace, do you know a Lord Lindworth?" Molly stopped beside her uncle's chair in his sitting room. It was a large room with white wainscoting and blue walls above the chair rail. The room was newly equipped with two blue chairs, a handsome walnut side table, and an ancient tapestry. The furniture had been delivered yesterday from Mrs. Wiley's. The tapestry looked splendid in a space between two arched windows that looked out across the open countryside.

Molly's uncle sat in a wing chair with his gouty foot propped up on a cushioned stool. Uncle Brace was nearly sixty, and his hair was thick and white. Woolly eyebrows stood like white caterpillars above clear blue eyes. He was not a large man, but he was solidly built, and when he spoke, his voice rang from deep inside his chest. Molly had always believed that he could be heard all the way to County Cork from County Down.

"Lord Lindworth?" Her uncle frowned, thought

a moment, then shook his head. "I do not know the name. Why do you ask?"

"We have received a letter from him by special messenger saying he will call tomorrow."

Her uncle smiled. "Well, now, that is pleasant news."

Antonia looked up from a desk nearby where she was laboring diligently over an extravagant Celtic letter C. She frowned. "Will you look at this, Molly, and tell me what I am doing wrong?"

Molly went to stand over the child. When Molly was a girl, Uncle Brace had encouraged her interest in illuminated manuscripts, and he had taught her calligraphy. She had become so good that she was sought by priests seeking to restore precious old manuscripts they found in the cellars of ancient churches.

"Just a bit lighter on the edges, Antonia. That will make the center look even darker." Molly took the pen and demonstrated on a piece of paper. With quick, agile lines she drew a C and then traced in the face of a centaur peeking from the middle. "There."

"Thank you." Antonia shook back her long hair and looked up at her cousin. "May we walk the dog later?"

"Of course." Molly returned to her uncle's side.

"It is kind of this Lord Lindworth to call," he said. "We have had few callers."

"You are not well enough to receive visitors yet. When you are better, people will come." At least Molly hoped they would, but she had been surprised that no one had called in the three weeks they had been in England. Her uncle had been born in Bath and had spent his boyhood here. Molly had assumed he would be welcomed back after living abroad all these years, but no invitations had appeared on the silver salver that waited on the handsome oak table beside the front door. In Ireland people would have called by now. But England and the English were different, she was learning.

"You must make certain we have some of the cook's cakes fresh for tomorrow."

"Yes, Uncle." It was not like Uncle Brace to concern himself about such details. Since their arrival in England, however, he had seemed anxious, and he fretted over things that never would have mattered to him before.

"You will see to the cakes now?" he pressed.

"Yes." Molly left, closing the big door behind her. She headed downstairs to talk with the cook about what to serve their guest tomorrow.

Although Molly was not impressed by titles, she was touched by Lord Lindworth's kindness at paying a call. No doubt he was an aging man who had known her uncle as a boy, and the two men might reminisce over sherry. Molly was touched by that thought.

Chapter 2

THE NEXT day before teatime, Molly donned a striped sarcenet gown of green and gold. She dressed without assistance. Molly's maid had remained in Ireland, and while in England, Molly shared with Antonia a maid named Frances. Molly had not bothered to ring for her this morning.

Antonia spent much of her time with her father. Because he had no son, he lavished the time and attention on his daughter that would have gone to a male heir.

Molly pulled her long red hair back into a loose chignon. Long hair, Molly knew, was not fashionable in England, but she did not care. She liked her hair flying loose when she ran down the hills with the dogs galloping around her, and she liked to comb it until it glistened in the firelight. Let the stuffy English ladies wear their hair cropped like a peasant's if they wished; she had no intention of conforming to their ways. Besides, Daniel liked her hair long and flowing.

Daniel Ryan was the man who waited for her in Ireland. His property adjoined that of her parents, and he and Molly had known each other since childhood. They had ridden ponies together, chased each other across peat bogs, and listened to Sir Brace's pirate tales together. Daniel was not only handsome, he was kind of heart. He never liked being the bearer of bad news. When one of her puppies died, he had it quietly buried. She did not learn of the death until her mother told her.

A light tap sounded on her door, and Molly opened it. Antonia rushed into the room. Her eyes were round, and she glanced over her shoulder before slamming the door shut.

"What is wrong?" Molly asked with quick concern.

" 'Tis nothing," the young girl said breathlessly, "I just wanted to visit."

Molly was not deceived. "You have been reading your stories about ghosts and vampires again."

"I am not frightened from anything I have been reading," she denied. "I am overwhelmed because the house is so large and I feel lost in it."

Kindred Manor was indeed bigger than any family needed. All that gray stone and windows on the outside and all these rooms inside. The first floor alone had private rooms in the south front, a suite of state rooms to the north, an oval antechamber, a state dressing room, a drawing room, and a saloon. That did not even include the ballroom that stretched across the back of the house. There were three more floors above. Even if one considered that the servants occupied the whole of the top floor, that still left a great deal of space.

Molly's own suite consisted of a cavernous dressing room, a sitting room, and her bedchamber. The four-poster bed draped with gossamer curtains was dwarfed in the corner of her large rose-colored chamber.

"I am glad to have you stay and talk with me,

22

but I shall be leaving in a minute to join our company." Crossing to the black trunk with the pretty gold designs that stood open in a corner, Molly began searching for her new white fan.

"Did you know a ghost haunts Lord Bryon's home?" Antonia asked. "It has been seen by all the servants." She knelt beside Molly and peered into the trunk.

Molly smiled at her. "You *have* been reading your gothic tales again."

Antonia tossed back her red hair. With a hauteur possessed only by one who is thirteen years old, she said, "Well, I do want to know what goes on in the world."

"Or what goes on in some writer's imagination." On a gentler note Molly added, "If you become frightened tonight, you know you can get into bed with me."

"I know." Antonia flushed, embarrassed to admit she sometimes needed to crawl into bed with Molly to calm her racing fears. After reading *Dismal Mansion* three months ago, she had spent the next two weeks in Molly's bed.

Antonia bounded to her feet. "You look very pretty, Molly. Pity 'tis wasted on the creaking old man who is coming. Still, glad I am that he is coming. It will make Papa happy to see one of his old friends." Pausing, Antonia inclined her head thoughtfully. "Papa said he could not remember this man. Do you find that passing strange? I remember the name of everyone who has ever been my friend."

Molly smiled. "When you are as old as your father, you may forget some things, too."

Antonia flitted around the room before stopping

beside a delicate mirror rimmed in silver that hung behind the door. With her index finger, she traced the oval of the mirror. "Why don't people come to see Papa? Why did he leave England in the first place?"

Molly tucked a loose curl behind her ear and dug deeper into the trunk for her fan. "I have been in England three weeks. I have watched the English riding about in their salon chairs, and they never deign to speak. The only wonder is that Uncle Brace did not leave earlier. Ah, here it is." Molly emerged with the fan. One feather hung bedraggled and broken, and Molly plucked it out.

Antonia darted to Molly's side. "I think Papa is afraid of something now that he is back. Have you noticed? It is not like Papa to fear anything. He was not even afraid when I told him the house in Ireland was haunted."

Molly walked to her writing desk near a casement window, and Antonia followed. "He is only a wee bit irritable because of his gout." Molly picked up a pen and drew the shape of an *L*, then playfully added a lamb peeking out from behind it.

Antonia took the pen and added the face of a witch poking out from the other side.

"Little minx. Your imagination is too vivid."

They were interrupted by a knock on the door and a female servant who reported, "The visitors have arrived. They have been shown to the drawing room."

Molly had expected only one person. Perhaps the man's wife had come, too. "Thank you," Molly said. "Please send word to Uncle Brace."

"Begging your pardon, ma'am, but your uncle is,

24

ah, indisposed, and the butler deemed it advisable not to disturb him."

Antonia leaned against her and whispered, "That means Papa has drunk too heavily."

Molly sighed. In trying to dull the pain of the gout, Uncle Brace did sometimes fall into his cups. The result was that he did not always come to dinner. At other times he could be heard singing in loud, slurred words.

Antonia wickedly sketched a wineglass in the witch's hand.

Molly gave her a reproving look, but she was more concerned with the guests. It was now going to fall to her to entertain them. What did she have to say to two old people who had known her uncle years ago?

She looked wistfully out the window at the cloudless blue sky. What a fine day to explore the next valley with Antonia and the dog. Or drive with Antonia to the shops. There were a dozen things she would rather do.

"Are you leaving now?" Antonia asked.

"Yes. Are you afraid to stay by yourself then?" If Antonia was afraid, Molly did not want to leave her alone. It was not, of course, as interesting as spending time with her father. He showed her rare illuminated manuscripts that had been penned by Irish monks centuries ago. Uncle Brace added spice to his lectures by telling of bloody battles and the monks' daring escapes from bloodthirsty Vikings. The tales were not suitable for a young girl, Molly knew, but they were the same stories that had enthralled her when she was younger.

"I am fine. I will go to my room to finish the page

25

I am working on. I think my hand is getting better. The A's look quite elegant," she said proudly.

"Good. I'll be wanting to see them." Molly touched her cousin's cheek affectionately, then started out the door to see to the guests. Her fingertips skimmed the white banister as she went down the curving steps. Then she walked down a wide hall punctuated by long windows toward the drawing room. As she walked, she admired the pretty new gold wall sconces that bracketed several new landscape paintings. The decoration added much to the bare green walls. Of course, there was still a great deal to be done in furnishing a house this size, but Molly had made an excellent start with the things she had bought from Mrs. Wiley.

Uncle Brace could order additional furniture made. Once his gout was better, he could even go to London to buy some at auction.

Molly reached the open double doors of the drawing room and stepped inside. Two men stood beside the unlit fireplace of veiny Italian marble. She looked at them and hesitated. Both were young and fashionably dressed. Some might call the men handsome, although their features were too precisely chiseled for her taste. She liked a man with a bolder, more carefree appearance—like Daniel Ryan. One could tell at a glance these men had valets who kept them perfectly attired. She wondered how they knew Uncle Brace, then decided that did not signify. It was enough that they had come to call on him.

The taller man saw her. She thought she detected a flicker of surprise, as if she was not what he had expected, but not an unwelcome sight. Then his face closed over to an impassive mask, the slate gray eyes revealing nothing.

Smiling, she started forward. "I am Miss Mills. My uncle is feeling unwell and is not able to join us. Sure 'tis a disappointment to him. He sends his deepest regrets."

The taller one stepped forward. "I am Lord Lindworth. This is my brother, Mr. Henry Cambridge."

After the niceties of introductions had been observed, she said, "Please sit down. I shall have tea and cakes brought up." Molly was glad the four striped chairs flanking the tea table had arrived yesterday. Without them, the room would have been almost bare. The Aubusson rug centered on the parquet floor was also a new addition. She noticed the earl looking at it closely. Admiring it, no doubt.

"Thank you, but I am afraid this is not a social call," Lord Lindworth said.

"Oh?" Molly looked at his somber face and tried to imagine what the earl might look like with his hair unkempt from a wild ride. She failed to conjure up a picture. He seemed so stiff, so proud, so very English.

Lord Lindworth looked at the rug again. "There has been a mistake, you see."

"Yes, we have come all the way from our home north of London looking for our property," the younger one said. "We lost it, but now we have found it again."

It was such a perfectly ludicrous statement that Molly stared, then began to giggle.

The earl lifted his head and squared his shoulders, as if preparing for battle. "I am at a loss to

27

understand why you are amused. To begin with, this is my rug," he said crossly.

"Your rug?" His hair was clipped to à la Brutus perfection. He looked arrogant, humorless, and boring. It was because of people like him that she was returning to Ireland. Still, she had not thought even the English were so overbearing as this. For him to come into her uncle's home and treat her as if she were a servant was appalling. She was on the point of saying so when the younger one spoke again.

"Everything you bought from Mrs. Wiley was stolen from our house by the gypsy I left in charge," he explained.

Molly stared from one to the other. They must both be in their cups. She had seen gypsies in Ireland. They were tinkers who came to the back door of the house and mended pots. One did not leave a gypsy in charge of one's house. Ever.

"He was to oversee the estate, but he and a few of his fellows departed with several cartloads of possessions. So you see, the furniture really belongs to us, and you will have to return it." Mr. Cambridge tried to soften his words with a smile. "We will send someone to fetch everything tomorrow."

Molly stared at the face of the taller one. What were they talking about? This furniture belonged to her uncle. "It has been paid for by Sir Brace," she said shortly.

"Then I fear you have lost your money," Lord Lindworth said. "You should have investigated more carefully before purchasing from someone like Mrs. Wiley. Surely you questioned how she came by such valuable stock?"

Molly's temper began to simmer. These men had

left a gypsy in charge of their property and had the effrontery to question *her* judgment?

"You see, it really is very simple. You have bought our furniture, and you are obliged to give it back to us." It was the younger one speaking—the one who kept smiling and acting as if he wished to be her friend. He was not as handsome as Lord Lindworth, but he did seem more pleasant. Laughter might be possible in those eyes. The earl's cold gray eyes suggested he did not know how to laugh.

"While he was managing the estate during the illness of our regular overseer, Mr. Stinson, he took some of the property and sold it." Mr. Cambridge spread his hands in a helpless gesture as if inviting her sympathy.

She glanced at the chairs and table, then down at the rug. She thought of the sconces gleaming golden on the walls, and the furniture in her uncle's room. She recalled how pleased Uncle Brace had been with everything. She also reflected that she had gone to a deal of time and trouble finding, purchasing, and arranging delivery of the items.

"I'm sure I cannot see what that has to do with me." Her voice was husky from the strain of holding her temper in check. "If you were so daft as to leave your family home in the hands of a scoundrel, you must live with the consequences, don't you see. Besides," she added as a brisk afterthought, "how do I know you are who you claim to be?"

The younger one's mouth gaped open while Lord Lindworth's jaw hardened into a tense line. The silence in the room crackled. Molly thought Lord Lindworth's eyes looked like the Irish Sea before a storm—gray and foreboding.

Finally Lord Lindworth asked in a tight voice,

"Is there someone else I could speak with?" He was used to being obeyed, Molly thought. He did not know her very well if he thought she cared a fig that he was displeased.

Molly studied him and entertained the idea of letting him speak to Uncle Brace. Her uncle would either swear at him or throw a drunken arm around the earl's arrogant neck. Either way, she thought Lord Lindworth would be horrified.

The earl drew himself up to a height that was impressive even in the high-ceilinged room. "If you refuse to cooperate, Miss Mills, it may be necessary for me to call in the Bow Street Runners."

"The Bow Street Runners operate in London," she said frostily. Just because she had an Irish accent did not mean she did not know what went on in the rest of the world.

"There are authorities here I could speak with," he snapped.

Molly brushed aside bothersome tendrils of hair that had floated free of her chignon. "I daresay there are. However, I have proof I paid for these items. What proof do you have that they ever belonged to you? Do you have a bill of sale showing when you bought them?"

"Of course not. They have been in my family for generations. Whatever bills of sale may have originally existed are gone."

"Pity." Her unsympathetic glare was at odds with the word.

Lord Lindworth sighed. "It does not appear that we are making any progress, Miss Mills."

"No, we are not." She did not blink under his murderous gaze. He might be a lord, but he was not going to order her about as if she were a scullery maid. He was in her uncle's home, and he was acting as if she should obey him. She had not the least intention of doing so.

After a few moments of tense silence, Lord Lindworth jammed his curly-brimmed hat onto his head and started for the door. "I shall give you time to reflect on this. You may depend on it that you will hear from me again."

"Do reconsider, Miss Mills," Mr. Cambridge said in a friendlier tone. He bowed to her just before they disappeared through the double doors.

"Insufferable man." She was thinking of the earl. Defiantly she sat down in the chair he claimed was his. If he wished to summon the authorities, so much the better. She had the stronger case. Until he could prove the objects were his, *and* until he paid for them, she was not giving up anything. They could take her to gaol if they wished.

Molly jumped up and paced the drawing room. Then she stormed out of the house and marched around the garden. The more she thought about events, the more it stoked her anger.

It was in the garden that the butler found her sometime later. He was an elderly butler who had come with them from Ireland. "Your uncle requests your presence." His shoulders were stooped, but he held the rest of himself with a military bearing.

"Is Uncle Brace feeling better?" she asked delicately.

The servant avoided her gaze. "I believe so." Old Thomas was stubbornly loyal to his master and would never admit his master was drunk.

"Thank you."

Her striped skirts fluttered around her as Molly started down the hall to her uncle's suite on the

31

main floor. He had selected these rooms because he had not felt equal to the challenge of climbing stairs to the second-floor bedrooms.

As she walked toward his room, she debated what she would say. Her uncle would want a report on the visit, of course. It was not Molly's habit to avoid the truth, but while Uncle Brace was plagued with gout, she did not like to add to his concerns by telling him the true purpose of the call.

Molly found her uncle sitting up in bed in his large room. The drawn curtains made the room dim, but she could still see that his face was red and blotchy. The scent of liquor permeated the room. The bedclothes were rumpled as if from a restless sleep.

"I understand my guests have been here." His words sounded like an accusation, but Molly knew his deep voice made everything sound that way.

She sat on a chair beside the bed and said calmly, "We did not think you were well enough to receive them."

He stirred, scowled, then sank back and grinned ruefully. The blue eyes twinkled beneath the white, woolly eyebrows. "I drink too much to soothe the ache in my foot, and then I sleep and wake up with an ache in my head. I daresay I shall have to give up the drinking and endure the gout."

"That might be wise."

"Well, then, what did they say, lass?"

Molly tried for evasion. "Lord Lindworth came with his brother. They were rather formal and did not stay long."

He laughed. "You must accustom yourself to the fact the English are reserved. Of course they were formal. What did they speak about?"

Molly busied herself readjusting the pins in her chignon and smoothing a wrinkle from her skirt. "They noticed the furnishings. They may have mentioned the weather; I cannot recall. They were only here a short time."

"How curious." He sank back in the big, bolstered bed, his white hair disappearing into the white pillows.

She rose quickly. "You are fatigued. I will leave you to your rest."

He ignored that. "You must invite them for dinner."

Molly halted in midstride. Dinner? And serve them on what they would insist were their plates?

"Did they say how they knew me?"

"By reputation," she blurted for want of anything else to say.

He sighed and closed his eyes. "Ah."

Molly stared in surprise. It was as if her uncle had expected her to say those words, and hearing them confirmed something for him. He looked tired and sad.

She returned slowly to his side and touched his blue-veined hand as it lay at the edge of the bed. "Is something wrong, Uncle Brace?"

He opened his eyes and smiled wanly. "Nothing. Why don't you and Antonia go for a walk while the weather is still nice? Or she may need help with her calligraphy. You know the trouble she sometimes has. But she will improve; she is determined, just like you were."

"You are changing the subject."

He smiled. "I thought I did so rather handily."

"You did so badly, but I will not press you."

33

"There's a good girl. I shall see you at dinner-time."

As she pulled the door closed behind her, Molly wondered what secret her uncle was keeping.

Lord Lindworth had once traveled to Ireland, he reflected as he sat in the clubroom of Rigley's mulling over his earlier visit with Molly Mills. Beside him Lord Sampler enjoyed wine from the club's fine cellar while Lawrence brooded. Lawrence had found the weather in Ireland disagreeable, the roads deplorable, and the people too plainspoken. Miss Mills was just another example of what was wrong with Ireland.

Granted, she was comely. He had always preferred blue-eyed women, but her green eyes and long lashes were fetching. The red wisps of hair that had fought free from the pins had danced around her fragile face. She had looked like an angel, but it was clear she was more like the opposite.

For one thing, she did not know how to conduct herself. A lady should be demure and shy. When addressed by an earl, she should respond in quiet tones.

Molly Mills had an Irish accent that kept the words floating up and down, and she had a way of looking directly at him. The fact she was probably at this minute sitting defiantly in a chair that belonged to him only made him more irritable toward her.

"She sounds a saucy chit," Lord Sampler said. The clubroom was dark with oak paneling. Even the fireplace was of black marble. The smells of fine whiskey and leather boots, and the pungent odor of cheroots, all made it a very masculine room. No woman had ever been admitted here, although women were frequently discussed.

Lord Lindworth grunted. He had known the Marquis of Sampler since both were at Harrow. Before that, their mothers had been friends.

"I have not seen Molly Mills m'self, but I hear she is a prime article," Sampler said.

Lord Lindworth was not about to compliment the vixen. "If one cares for that sort," he muttered.

"Her uncle left here many years ago. Went to Ireland. A scandal, as I recall. He married an Irish woman of no birth. I am surprised he has come back. He has money, though," Sampler continued. "Enough to buy that old pile that went to auction when Banford died. The house was empty of furniture, though, so it stands to reason they would have to buy some."

"I do not object to them buying furniture," Lord Lindworth snapped. "I object to them buying *mine*."

"What are you going to do?" the marquis inquired lethargically. He had been trim and athletic and a demon on the playing fields when Lawrence had known him at Harrow. Now he had a round stomach and a second chin. His smile was still contagious, however, and he always had the fanciest of high-flyers in keeping in London. Alas, he was not always prompt in the payment of his bills, and he was in Bath rusticating until the angry tradesmen subsided.

"I am not sure." Lord Lindworth had threatened her with the authorities, but the truth was, he did not wish to bring such attention to himself. He preferred handling the affair in a more discreet manner. "What about her uncle?" Lawrence asked his friend. "Perhaps he is a man of reason." Although

35

going to Ireland and marrying an Irishwoman did nothing to confirm that hope.

"The uncle?" Lord Sampler stirred himself to ask lazily.

"Yes. Is he invited out? If I could meet him under better circumstances, I could talk to him as one gentleman to another. I could certainly make more headway with him than with his niece."

Lord Sampler took a maddening amount of time to finish the dregs in his glass, wipe his mouth with his fingers, and tap his chin thoughtfully. "I have not seen him anywhere. Did I mention there was a scandal?"

"Yes, but you did not say what it was about."

"What an unfriendly tone, Lawrence. You are out of patience with everyone. I do hope you do not snap at the prince like that when he comes to visit you."

Lawrence took a deep breath and asked again, "Do you know what the scandal concerned?"

Sampler shrugged his big shoulders. "I have no idea. Whatever it was is ancient now. The young lady's uncle has been away above thirty years."

Lord Lindworth considered that. What in the devil could the man have done that kept him from being invited about after thirty years? It was dashed inconvenient for Lawrence that Sir Brace was not received in the overheated, dowager-infested salons of Bath. At least then Lawrence could speak with him under more cordial circumstances.

There was nothing for it, he decided. He must return to Kindred Manor and demand to speak to the man. He was not leaving Bath without his property, and he did not intend to remain any longer than he must.

That resolution made, Lawrence joined Lord Sampler in a glass of port. Afterward they both repaired downstairs to the back parlor to enjoy a game of faro.

The very next morning, Lawrence prepared to return to Sir Brace's house. He stopped at Henry's room, determined that his brother should be as inconvenienced as he.

His brother's room was furnished with richly waxed dark pieces of furniture. Even though the windows were open to admit the morning light, the brown flock paper made the room murky. Samuel, the crisp young valet, greeted Lawrence deferentially at the door.

"Tell Henry I wish to see him."

"He is out at the moment, milord."

Lawrence could see the valet examining his clothes and giving mute approval to the job Lawrence's own man had done with the claret morning coat, short trousers, and simply tied cravat. Clothes were not of importance at the moment. "Where is he?"

"He went to the theater last night, milord."

Lawrence arched a sardonic eyebrow. "Met an actress, did he?"

"Well, there was a young lady." Samuel, who had shown no sign of a cold previously, coughed delicately. "He took a hackney cab. It might have broken down, and he might have been unable to return here and might have been obliged to spend the night away."

Blast Henry. The cawker had made a muddle of things, and now he was out spending his allowance on women he could not afford and was probably not yet accomplished enough to satisfy.

The earl had given up actresses half a dozen years ago. That was not to say he was a saint, but he was particular in his taste in women. As far as a wife, no woman had presented herself who met his exacting standards. He would require a woman of impeccable breeding, possessed of a suitable dowry, and conscious of his position as head of the household. A lady who was demure and obedient. He would not object if she was also a blue-eyed beauty.

"Shall I send someone in search of Mr. Cambridge?" the valet asked.

"That will not be necessary." It would only waste time. He would go to Kindred Manor alone.

There, fifteen minutes later, he was met at the door by the same butler as before. He presented his card with the clipped announcement, "I wish to speak to Sir Brace immediately. It is on a matter of utmost importance."

Out of the corner of his eye, he noticed a young girl hovering at the top of the stairs.

"If you will wait here, please," the servant said in a heavy Irish brogue. It lacked the musical, lilting quality of Molly Mills's voice, the earl noted, and was annoyed with himself for finding anything pleasant about the woman.

The Irish butler turned and disappeared down a hall. Lord Lindworth looked up to see the young girl peering at him through the banister rails. She flushed when she realized he was looking at her. Even the children had no notion of how to go on, he thought.

The butler returned. "Follow me, please."

Instead of returning to the drawing room where he had gone yesterday, Lawrence found himself trailing down a maze of halls that ended at a sitting room.

A man was seated in front of a fireplace. He had white hair and thick white eyebrows. He smiled greetings from a large red wing chair. A matching chair sat across from it.

"Come in, come in, lad. I'm Sir Brace. Can't stand on ceremony. Can't stand at all." He laughed heartily. "Gout. Very bad case of it. Do come in and sit down."

Lord Lindworth refused to be swayed to sympathy by the illness. Sir Brace, he noted, was seated in a chair that had been in Wicklowe Hall's small parlor for over a hundred years. It should be there right now.

Lawrence sat down across from the white-haired man. "I shall go directly to the point, sir. I am certain your niece told you about our discussion yesterday."

Sir Brace smiled disarmingly. "I confess she did not. Have a glass of this fine Madeira and we can talk more amiably. You seem anxious."

Lawrence stared at his host. "She did not tell you?"

"No need to shout. It's my foot that doesn't work, not my ears."

Lawrence accepted the glass the butler thrust into his hand. In a quieter voice he repeated, "Your niece did not explain to you that I came to recover my property?"

"No. Try the Madeira. It will calm you."

Jumping up, Lawrence paced about. "I do not want to be calm. I am here to talk about my possessions." He ranged about the room, stalking from the floor-to-ceiling windows, past the bookcases, and back to the chairs. As he moved, he told the old man exactly what he had told Molly yesterday. He concluded with, "The Prince Regent is to arrive at my house inside of two months. I do not intend for him to find a bare house. Everything must be returned immediately."

Sir Brace had listened throughout with a bemused expression. Now he cocked his head and asked, "Did you say the Prince Regent will be at your house?"

"Indeed I did." What was the matter with these people? he wondered in exasperation. Did they not attend to anything he said?

"Mmmm."

"So you can see the urgency of regaining my property. I tried to make all this clear to your niece, but she failed to understand." Lawrence made it plain by his tone that if Sir Brace also failed to understand, there would be unhappy consequences.

"She is only a woman," Sir Brace lowered his voice to confide.

The conspiratorial air took Lawrence aback. "Then you will not try to present obstacles?"

"Of course not!" Sir Brace looked offended. "As a matter of fact, I will do my utmost to have everything returned as quickly as possible. With the prince coming to visit, naturally you want everything to be perfection."

"Yes, I do." Thank heavens he had met a man with sense. It did seem, however, that his host was studying him rather shrewdly. Lawrence dismissed that notion. Sir Brace was acting as a gentleman should. It was because Lawrence had come prepared to fight that he could not believe everything had been resolved so easily.

"You are friends with the Prince Regent?" Sir Brace was half-hidden behind his glass, swirling the Madeira and watching the earl.

"Yes."

"I see."

In the silence that followed, Lord Lindworth felt compelled to say, "The prince and I share an interest in architecture. We have met on a number of occasions, but it is the first time he has honored us with a visit to our home."

"Yes, yes, an honor indeed."

Lord Lindworth still had the uneasy feeling something was going on inside Sir Brace's head. "I daresay we should talk about how we can arrange to have my property returned."

"Yes, let us talk about that."

Chapter 3

"THAT MAN who was here yesterday is downstairs."

Molly looked up from adding a lace collar to her blue satin gown to where a breathless Antonia stood in the doorway twisting a lock of her disheveled red hair. Her pink muslin gown had thistles on the hem and a streak of mud down one side, probably acquired when the dog jumped on her.

"He was standing in the hallway tapping his walking stick against his knee and looking thoroughly unhappy. He frowned at me," Antonia added. "He asked to speak to Papa."

Molly made a face. "Drat. I was afraid he would not remain away." She was still in the amber-colored morning dress she had worn earlier. She and Molly had gone to an antiquarian bookstore and perused the shelves for something of suitable condition and beauty to interest Uncle Brace. They had discovered a good copy of Mr. Johnson's book and had purchased it, intending to present it to him to cheer him.

Now the disagreeable earl was here to cause more trouble and probably make Uncle Brace's humor and gout even worse.

"Perhaps I can stop him before he meets with

42

Uncle," Molly said, and hurried out of the room and down the steps. As she moved through the halls, her amber skirts swinging out behind her, she regretted again a house of such size that it took ages to go from one floor to the next.

Her uncle's house in Ireland had been well appointed but modest in size. Molly had been startled when she first saw Kindred Manor. It was as if her uncle was trying to impress someone. Yes, there were castles like that in Ireland. Birr Castle had elegant Waterford crystal chandeliers, and Glin Castle in County Limerick stretched beautifully along the River Shannon. Although her family had money, they lived more simply. Uncle Brace had, too.

Since coming to England, though, he was acting differently. She had never known him to be secretive before, but now it appeared there was something he had kept from her.

Molly reached the drawing room and looked inside the open door. No one there. She hurried on to her uncle's sitting room. As she neared it, she heard men's voices.

At least they were not shouting, she consoled herself. Molly paused in the doorway. The two men sat facing each other in front of a dwindling fire. Molly looked at her uncle's face and was relieved to see he did not seem overset.

Her uncle spied her and grinned with more enthusiasm than she had seen in some time. "Ah, Molly. You remember our guest, Lord Lindworth?"

The earl rose and executed a stiff bow.

Remember him? Of course she did; one did not forget a man who was so thoroughly unpleasant.

"Come in, come in. Sit down, Molly," her uncle said expansively.

She sat on a side chair and looked from one man to the other. What had happened so far? Both men seemed in good humor. Had Lord Lindworth not yet explained the purpose of his visit? Or was Uncle Brace too far into his cups to be perturbed by anything? She looked at her uncle and saw that he was perfectly sober.

"Lord Lindworth informs me there has been a grievous error concerning how we came into possession of our new furniture. Once I learned the truth, I naturally assured him we would return everything."

Molly stared in astonishment. It was not like her uncle to give in so easily. Had his gout robbed him of his spirit? Whatever the reason, she could not allow him to concede to this ridiculous demand. "Uncle Brace, you'll not be wanting to give it back after the trouble we went to and—"

"Now, child, do not interrupt. It would appear Mrs. Wiley sold you stolen merchandise. Terrible, terrible." He paused to shake his head mournfully at the travesty.

"They included some of my family's priceless treasures." Lord Lindworth kept his eyes on her uncle, but she knew the accusatory words were meant for her.

"All the more reason we must right this error!" Sir Brace paused for a phlegmy cough, then continued, "The furnishings are too precious to be given into the care of just anyone. I shall take great pains in how they are transported back; you have my word on that, my lord."

"Thank you. You are a man of great understanding."

Molly's uncle nodded and continued, "As I was saying, I would as lief pluck out my eyes as have any

44

damage come to your property. I do not do things by half measures, you will be gratified to know."

"That is very kind of you, sir." The earl looked comfortable and self-satisfied sitting by the fireplace with one knee crossed over the other. His empty glass sat on the small table beside him.

Molly glared at him, but he either did not notice or he did not care. How could Uncle Brace give in so readily?

"Indeed, I shall oversee the return of your property myself," her uncle continued. "It is the least I can do for the inconvenience you have been caused."

Molly had only the briefest image of the earl blinking in surprise before she turned her own quizzical expression on her uncle. "Sure and you cannot mean to journey to Lord Lindworth's home, Uncle Brace? You are not well enough to make such a trip."

He waved her to silence. "I know my duties, lass."

"Sir Brace," the earl began, "that is kind of you, but I do not expect—"

The older man held up a silencing hand. "Let us hear no more argument on this head." Softening, he smiled. "If you are concerned for my health, Lord Lindworth, fear not. I shall bring my niece and daughter with me. They will look after me, and it is a splendid way for them to see England. I am especially pleased that my niece be able to do so since she will soon be returning to Ireland."

The earl no longer looked smug. The gray eyes fixed on her uncle were distrustful. He brushed a hand through his short, dark hair and cleared his throat. "I really cannot ask this of you. I live a great distance from here. It is further away than London."

"I insist. Here, Molly, pour our guest some more Madeira. His glass is empty. There's a good girl."

Molly rose and took the heavy crystal decanter from near the bookcase and started toward the earl. She was lifting the decanter to pour into his glass when she was struck by a revelation. Uncle Brace had found a way to get his family admitted into one of the best houses in England. The fact Molly had no wish to go and the fact the earl did not want them were of no importance to her uncle.

Sir Brace was waxing expansive about the last time he had been north of London. "It has been a number of years, but I fancy the roads have not changed so much as all that." He smiled over at Molly. "We shall start as soon as arrangements can be made."

"All the furnishings must be returned quickly." Lord Lindworth's voice had taken on a less genial tone.

Molly debated pouring the liquor over the earl's head. But it was some of Uncle Brace's finest from the wine cellar, and it was a shame to waste perfectly good wine.

"I know you need everything back before the prince arrives. When did you say he is coming?"

"The first weekend in September."

"That long from now," her uncle mused. "We shall definitely have everything back by then, won't we, Molly?"

She nodded, not trusting herself to speak. She was caught between dismay and the urge to laugh. Take that, your lordship. He had insisted on getting his furniture back, but it was coming at a high cost.

"Molly, you haven't yet poured our guest his drink."

46

"I do not want anything." The earl rose abruptly. "I cannot impose further on your hospitality. I have other matters I must attend to. Thank you."

"Quite welcome. My niece will see you to the door. I am grateful to you for bringing this unfortunate situation to my attention. I am pleased I can be of help." Uncle Brace beamed broadly. His cheeks were even rosier than usual, and his eyes sparkled.

Molly started out the door with the earl behind her. His boots made loud thumping noises on the gleaming black and white tile. She suspected annoyance made his steps even heavier. Her own footsteps were faint whisking sounds muffled by her flowing skirts. They walked down the hallways without speaking.

When they reached the front doorway, she turned to him. "Has everything been arranged to your satisfaction then?" She kept her face serenely composed.

He looked at her hard. She was sure he knew her question was meant to nettle. "I shall be glad to recover what is mine," was all he said before accepting his walking stick from Old Thomas and jamming the stick under his arm. He left the house.

Molly watched him through the window as he mounted his horse. It was dreadful to be in agreement with the earl on anything, but she did hope Uncle Brace decided not to make such a trip. She had no wish to go. What was more, she thought Uncle Brace would be disappointed if he thought to gain a foothold into English society through the earl. Lord Lindworth was a callous, uncaring man who would not extend himself to help anyone, least of all her uncle.

Over the next few days, Lawrence wondered if a curse had fallen over him. As he dragged Henry back toward Wicklowe Hall, the carriage broke an axle and they were forced to take lodgings at the slovenly Brine and Burly. Lord Lindworth had never seen linens of such a distasteful shade of gray before.

Once they were riding again, strong winds slowed their progress. They also whipped up clouds of dust that found their way in through the closed windows of the carriage. Every time the earl opened his mouth to talk, he tasted grit.

At last they arrived back at Wicklowe Hall only to be greeted by the butler with the news their mother was returning home early and would arrive in the morning.

" 'S blood," Henry mumbled.

"Blast" was Lawrence's contribution. As if he did not have enough other concerns. He was tired, but he could not allow himself the luxury of rest. He had lost far too much time already, and he had far too much to do.

"This also arrived for you." The butler stood in the empty hall and impassively presented him a missive bearing the royal seal.

Lawrence opened it and scanned quickly.

"What does it say?" Henry demanded as he read over Lawrence's shoulder.

"That he hopes I have plans ready for him to look at when he arrives."

"Very flattering, that last bit," Henry said, and quoted, " 'I know I can depend on you. You are certain to have several excellent designs ready for my perusal. I look forward to seeing them.' Have you anything for him to look at?"

"No," Lawrence barked. "When have I had time to work on them?" He was going to have a deal less time once his mother arrived. He could only imagine what she was going to say when she saw the state of the house.

Lady Lindworth had been a beauty when she was presented more seasons ago than she cared to acknowledge. She had married an earl and had proceeded to conduct herself as befitted her station by spending the Season in London and frequenting the fashionable watering holes with other women of quality. She had relied upon her husband to make all decisions and to see to her needs. Upon her husband's death, she had transferred responsibility for her well-being and happiness to her elder son. She was going to suffer a fit of apoplexy when she saw the house.

As it happened, Lawrence was asleep late the next morning when his mother's carriage rolled up the elm-lined drive to Wicklowe Hall. He had been up until the small hours of the morning working on sketches, and he had fallen asleep over his work. His concerned valet had awakened him and shepherded him into bed sometime very late.

Now his valet was back hovering over his bed and looking apologetic. "I am sorry to disturb you, milord, but your mother has arrived and requests your presence in her rooms."

Lawrence raised himself up on both elbows. Still groggy, he asked, "How long has she been here?"

"Only a short while, but she appears most, ah, eager to speak with you."

He swung himself over the edge of the bed, holding on to an exquisitely carved post with one hand. The bed was of such massive size that even the gypsies must have deemed it more trouble than it was worth to cart it from the house.

Through the open door of the dressing room, Lawrence could see the valet had already laid out a tan coat, brown doeskin trousers, and blucher boots for the day's wear. Sighing, he stood. He might as well dress and get this over with.

Fifteen minutes later, even though his cravat was not tied to his valet's satisfaction, Lawrence found his mother in her sitting room on the second floor. Its windows gave a view over the meadow. In the distance, beyond the green spires of trees, could be seen the steeple of the village church. The walls of the room were bedecked with hand-painted yellow roses. It was good the walls were colorful, for there was little else left in the room. The dainty chairs and pretty tables had all been taken. Lady Lindworth saw her son and rushed toward him.

"Thank heavens, Lawrence. I have been at sixes and sevens since I arrived."

His mother was a slight, pale woman. She had only a few white strands scattered among her shining black hair. He had no chance to give her an affectionate kiss on the cheek before her fingers dug frantically into his wrist.

"We have been robbed! The house is stripped of everything." She swept a pitiful look about the room. "All my beautiful chairs have vanished. This is the worst disaster that has ever befallen us."

"Mother, I know it is a shock, but it has all been recovered and is being returned."

"I do not know how I shall go on," she continued in a wail.

"Mother, you are not attending. We have located our property, and it is even now being carried back to us."

She blinked up at him. Slowly her fright was replaced by tears of relief. "It is? Oh, I knew you would know what to do." She wiped aside a tear and smiled wanly. "Thank goodness you are here to attend to matters."

He led her toward a bench seat built into the window ledge. It was the only place to sit left in the empty room. "Sit here until you have recovered yourself."

"Everything is being returned," she murmured to herself. She looked quickly up at him. "The ruby-encrusted goblets?"

"They were garnets, Mother, and Henry pried them out when he was a child."

"Oh, yes, of course. I had forgotten." She thought a moment longer. "When will the furnishings be back? The Prince of Wales is coming, you know."

"Yes, I do know," he said patiently. When she subsided quietly back against the window, he added, "We were obliged to go to Bath to find them."

"Bath! How dreadful for you. No one of any importance is there at this time of year. You must have been bored beyond endurance."

"We went there on a mission of recovering our possessions," he reminded her gently.

"Oh, yes." She touched her hand to her hair in a gesture he suspected she had learned as a coquette. Now she did it out of long habit. "Will everything be back today?"

"I doubt that."

"Tomorrow?"

He sighed. "I cannot say. A man named Sir Brace is overseeing the return himself."

Her attention was suddenly caught. "Whom did you say?"

"Sir Brace. He is newly returned to England from Ireland."

Her eyes became as large as plates. She did not blink. "You cannot mean it. I had heard he had returned, but I gave no thought to the matter. And you say he is coming *here*." She wrung her hands. "Oh, Lawrence, this will never do. We cannot have him in the house."

Lawrence tensed. While his mother was sometimes given to melodrama, he sensed she was earnest about this. "Why can he not come here?" he asked carefully.

Rising, she stirred around the room, stopping to touch a painted rose on the wall and rounding back to the windows. "He was banished from the country by the king himself. He was told never to return."

"Why was he banished?" Even as he asked, Lawrence suspected he did not want to know.

"The two men quarreled, and Sir Brace hit King George. He hit the king," she repeated, lest he fail to understand the enormous significance of that statement. "He bloodied King George's face."

Lawrence's spirits sank. So that was why Sir Brace had lived in Ireland all these years. He had allowed himself to be tricked into letting the man come to Wicklowe Hall. What *had* he been thinking to permit someone who was not invited to the most provincial fetes in Bath to come to his ancestral home?

His mother fixed him with pleading eyes. "It would be dreadful if anyone knew Sir Brace was welcomed here. I cannot bear to think of the disgrace." A handkerchief appeared from nowhere, and she twisted it in her fingers.

Lawrence did not like the idea of being outfoxed, but he clearly had been. The old schemer and his madcap niece must be laughing up their sleeves at the moment. Well, perhaps Miss Mills had not been a part of the machinations, he conceded, for she seemed to have no interest in coming here. He could see her still, challenging him with those clear green eyes.

"Lawrence, what shall we do?" his mother asked plaintively.

"We have no choice but to allow them here or we may not recover our property."

"Oh!"

Although, once in possession of their property, Lawrence reflected grimly, he was under no obligation to offer a roof to Sir Brace or his niece. Let them stay at the White Stag a night and then return to Bath. Their comfort was not his concern.

"Ring for some burnt feathers, my dear. I am certain I shall swoon at any moment."

The earl helped her to the bench seat and stood patting her hand.

"Sally Jersey will give me the cut direct once it becomes known Sir Brace was in our house. I shall never see the inside of Almack's again. Countess Lieven will never countenance such a thing either. Even sweet Emily Cowper will refuse to acknowledge me—"

He had heard enough. "Mother, let us find a chamber for you that still has a bit of furniture. Once you are rested, I am persuaded everything will look better." He was lying; he thought it would look equally unpromising hours from now.

She gazed up at him as if longing to believe him.

Forcing a smile, he said, "The furniture will be here soon, and we will figure a way out of this coil."

Lawrence was obliged to repeat that reassurance to his mother the next day and again the following day. With each day that passed, he was one day closer to the Prince Regent's visit. It was now six weeks before the visit, and he had much to do.

Lawrence tried to work on his architectural plans in the large study downstairs—the one that faced out over the back of the estate. Usually the occasional sight of deer in the park or the preening of the peacocks on the green lawn comforted him. Now, however, he found himself constantly tromping down the hall to throw the front door open and glare down the road that led up to the house. No carriage ever presented itself.

Where the devil was Sir Brace?

The waiting did little to soothe anyone's nerves. Even Henry showed signs of strain at dinner. Several times he offered to ride out in search of the party, but Lawrence refused to allow this. Henry was far better in his sight than out making mischief on the open road.

The housemaids scurried about cleaning windows inside and out, climbing up to the chandeliers to polish the brass, and spending endless hours waxing the floors. They tended to what little furniture remained, carefully cleaning it and preparing it for the royal visit.

Lady Lindworth took to her bed each afternoon. Lying in a darkened room with a damp cloth over her forehead, she was too distressed to do more than allow her dresser to read her the more shocking passages of Caro Lamb's book.

The whole household waited.

Antonia flitted around the room holding up gowns and unfolding garments the exasperated maid had just packed for Molly. Antonia dragged a blue slip of satin with a white patent net dress out of a trunk. "This will make you look a pretty coleen when you dance with the prince."

Molly made a wry face. "I'll not be dancing with the prince, and there's an end to it."

"Papa says you will. He says there will be ever so many entertainments and parties to attend and sweets to eat." Antonia giggled. "I would not like to dance, because I think it would be disagreeable to have some man put his hands on me, but I would enjoy the sweets."

Molly laughed. "When you are older it will make your heart flutter when certain men touch you."

"Never. What woman would want someone clammy and stiff like Lord Lindworth to touch her?"

"His hands were warm," Molly noted absently.

Antonia leaned in closer. "I think Wicklowe Hall is probably some creeping old pile with turrets like the rooks in a chess game and people locked in towers. Lord Lindworth no doubt prowls the halls at night meeting with agents of Napoleon and—"

"Really, Antonia."

"*You* don't like him either."

" 'Tis true I may not like him, but I have not built wild stories around him. He is going to be our host, reluctant though he may be in that duty."

Antonia made a face.

Molly turned her attention back to sorting clothes for the journey. She had thought they would start for Lord Lindworth's home soon after the earl left. Each day, however, Uncle Brace announced that his gout was improving, but he still was not well enough to travel.

Molly thought that odd, because his color was good and his spirits much improved. In fact, he did not seem to be in pain, but he insisted he was. She supposed he must be suffering, though, else why delay the trip? He was clearly anxious to go, because he had finagled their invitation.

Yet each day he postponed the trip. That meant Molly and Antonia had little to do but roam the countryside with the dog trotting after them. The cousins spent evenings and rainy afternoons in the cathedral-like library studying the ancient manuscripts they had brought with them and refining their skill at duplicating the letter-art of those manuscripts.

In Ireland few people thought it untoward for Molly to amuse herself in the nearly lost art. If she had been raised in England, though, Molly suspected she would have been forced to perfect her needlepoint or devote hours to gossip in the parlors and drawing rooms of friends. She would not have liked that.

Each time she touched the vellum of an illuminated manuscript, she felt history stir to life in her hands. She thought of the monks who had labored by the light of a single candle to create the manuscript. She remembered Uncle Brace's gripping stories about marauding savages attacking monasteries while terrified monks abandoned their precious creations in the flight to save their lives.

Molly had carefully packed a copy of an early

Gospel to take along with her to Wicklowe Hall. She was making a copy of it to present to a church in Galway to replace one of theirs that had been destroyed by fire. It was not the same as having an original, she knew, but it was better than nothing.

Besides, what else was she going to do with her time? She did not imagine Lord Lindworth was going to devote himself to entertaining her and her family. Even if he cared a fig about them, which he did not, he would be busy preparing for the prince's visit.

Uncle Brace had said they would only stay a day or two at Wicklowe Hall, so she would not have to endure the earl's presence long.

"Do you suppose Wicklowe Hall has ghosts?" Antonia asked.

The question startled Molly out of her reflections. She looked up to see her cousin leaning toward her. Smiling, she shook her head. "Of course not."

Antonia sighed. "You are probably right. Lord Lindworth would not allow his house to be haunted. He would stand in the hall in the middle of the night and cast stern looks at any ghosts that ventured out."

Molly laughed. "Do you really think he has that kind of power?"

"He certainly seemed capable of managing almost anything."

"He could not manage me," Molly said tartly. She would not have returned the furniture at all, and certainly not if the earl ordered her to instead of asking her politely. But that had been her uncle's decision to make, and she would abide by it. Still, it did not soften her attitude toward Lord Lindworth.

Chapter 4

TRAVELING UP from Bath did not prove to be so bad, although it was slow because of the three wagons piled high with furniture that followed their carriage down the roads. Molly had a guidebook to read about the areas they were passing through, and when she tired of that, Antonia read aloud from her latest gothic by Ann of Swansea. Uncle Brace, whose gout had mercifully ceased to trouble him, was in high good humor as he sat across from Antonia and Molly in the big traveling carriage. The maid Frances sat beside him.

When they grew bored, Molly and Antonia had amused themselves by choosing words to describe what they saw. "Crone," Antonia had said about an old woman drawing water from a well in a village they traveled through. "Grandmother," Molly had said more charitably.

"We shall be there within an hour," Sir Brace predicted with a cheerful look out the window.

Antonia glanced up from her book. "Do you think Lord Lindworth's house will have 'moldering walls and nodding watchtowers with sensations of horror'?"

"No, I think it will be a perfectly ordinary house.

58

Only a wee bit shy of furniture," Molly added with a wicked laugh.

"We are to be his guests," her uncle said, "so we must behave properly toward him."

"Of course," Molly said without remorse.

Uncle Brace leaned back and closed his eyes. "Read me more about the scenery, lass."

Molly opened the guidebook. "Chiltern Hills stretches some sixty miles northeast from the Thames at Goring to the Dunstable Downs. The hills are of chalk and unsuited to cultivation. Trees grow best. Open meadowland alternates with some of England's last true woods." Her uncle was already snoring as Molly closed the book and looked out the window.

The words on the page did not convey the full beauty of the hills and valleys. Of course, Ireland had richer and more varied shades of green, but she found the beech woods and fields of green rolling off into the distance charming, as was the little village they were just now driving through. Tall houses stared straight down into a stream that ran alongside the road through the center of town.

As they left the village behind and started back out into the countryside, Molly squinted into the distance at a clump of stone chimneys jutting up into the sky. A few moments later she saw a roofline. "There is some large building in the distance," she said.

Sir Brace opened his eyes. They rounded a curve in the road, and Molly saw a grand house sitting at the top of an incline. Rows of windows marched across the facade of the house like soldiers in formation. A gigantic archway framed what must be the main entrance at the center of the house.

"It is surely Wicklowe Hall," he said.

The house was impressive if formal, like the earl himself. As they drew nearer, Molly saw that it was built of gray stone with a gray slate roof. Gray smoke curled from a chimney. White capstones above the windows and doors lent a distinctive air to the mansion.

"Rambling," Antonia said.

"Our entree into society," Uncle Brace said.

Molly looked at him and saw excitement gleaming in his eyes beneath the white, woolly eyebrows. She had sensed his anticipation throughout the trip, but it was the first time that he had actually said aloud why it was so important to him to journey here. Molly did not question him about this, although she still thought it odd that a man with his title and money should need anyone's help to enter the drawing rooms of polite society.

Fifteen minutes later their large traveling carriage rolled to a halt in front of the house. While a servant let down the steps, the earl came out the front door. He glanced at them, then back at the road.

Molly could see he was worried about his precious furniture. Uncle Brace stepped down and helped her and Antonia alight.

"I hope you have plenty of men standing by," her uncle said heartily. "Three carts will be arriving soon."

Relief flooded the earl's face. "Since there is very little furniture in the house, I took the liberty of arranging accommodations for you at the local inn."

Her uncle waved the suggestion aside. "We are a rough breed. Little Antonia will not mind making shift for a day or two, and my niece Miss Mills is as hearty a chit as you have ever seen. Irish, you know, and the women there are sturdy. It will be fine for us to stay here."

The earl touched his perfectly starched cravat and tried again. "You see—"

"Won't be here more than a day or so." Sir Brace put a hand on the small of his back and rubbed. "We can talk later. The lasses are tired and I am stiff. The long trip has almost taken the pretty bloom off Molly's cheeks," he added with an affectionate glance toward her.

"Miss Mills looks lovely as always," Lord Lindworth said with perfunctory courtesy.

Molly adjusted her bonnet and flicked a look at her host. She did not think Lord Lindworth cared a whit about her coloring, although her red hair and fair skin with its spots of color high on each cheek had often excited comment among men before. Because this arrogant man was somehow important to her uncle, it would not serve to anger him. Molly dredged up a smile.

It might have been the smile that caused Lord Lindworth to pause. At any rate, he turned back to her uncle and said in resignation, "I shall order some rooms made ready. Please come into the house."

Sir Brace took his daughter's arm and started ahead. Lord Lindworth extended an elbow toward Molly.

As she put the tips of her fingers on his elbow, she saw his jaw was set at an angle of disapproval. He had been forced into allowing them to stay, and he did not like it.

"My uncle took great care with your furniture," she told him, a not-so-subtle reminder they had done the earl a great kindness. It was the least he could do to offer them hospitality for a day or two. Certainly they would not remain longer than that.

"I am pleased to hear it."

If he was truly pleased, it was more than she could detect in his cold manner and expression.

A short while later, Molly stood in the doorway of her room. The only furniture was a bureau and a small bed in the corner. That was enough for her needs, Molly reflected as she slipped out of her dark brown dress, pulled off the matching brown bonnet with its little nosegay of white ribbons at the side, and lay down to rest on the bed in her chemise. The journey had tired her, and she closed her eyes to rest.

She did not awaken until Antonia shook her some time later. Molly rose up and looked around the darkening room. "What time is it?"

"Time to dress for dinner."

Molly sank back against the pillow. "I must have slept hours. I didn't realize I was so tired."

"I have been watching the men working," Antonia informed her. "They have already unloaded almost everything. Furniture for this room is waiting out in the hall. The earl said you were not to be disturbed."

For that she was grateful. Molly pushed back her hair, which promptly fell forward again, framing her oval face in a nest of red curls. "I daresay I should find something to wear to dinner." She looked at Antonia's simple calico dress with a grass stain on the hem and added, "So should you."

Antonia hovered near the bed. "Do you think I should go to dinner with you? I do not know how such things are done in England."

"Of course you must." Molly did not like the thought of her cousin eating a solitary meal in her room or in the kitchen. In Ireland Antonia joined the family for dinner; that was exactly what she was going to do here. "Go along now and have Frances help you dress."

After the girl left, Molly donned a cambric frock of pale yellow that buttoned behind. The maid arrived to help her fasten the buttons. Then she swept Molly's hair back into a sensible braid that coiled around her head to form a crown. The maid even pulled the stray curls that usually flirted about Molly's face into a sleek cap.

Molly peered at herself in the mirror and murmured, "I look very serious and important." Good. She wanted the earl to know that she and her uncle were people to be reckoned with.

A knock sounded on the door, and Molly opened it to find Antonia waiting. "We are to meet in the drawing room. I have explored the house; I know where it is."

It was fortunate Antonia knew where to go. The long, polished corridors and myriad rooms were confusing to Molly. She followed her cousin past pictures of bygone earls and bejeweled countesses.

Uncle Brace was already in the drawing room when they arrived at the long room on the ground floor. Elegant white draperies shrouded the windows of the pale blue room. Uncle Brace was trussed up in a wine red waistcoat that showed signs of strain at the buttons. He looked well rested and in high spirits.

Lord Lindworth was also present. He was dressed in the height of fashion in a flawless claret red coat and white unmentionables. He rose when Molly and

63

Antonia entered the room. If he was surprised that Antonia joined them, he did not show it. "My mother was most grateful for the return of the furniture," he said. "She deeply regrets that she cannot join us for dinner. She has a megrim."

Molly did not find him a convincing liar. He said the words like an actor delivering himself of lines he had memorized only minutes before. His mother might have a headache, but Molly suspected it was because of their visit.

"Not joining us for dinner?" Uncle Brace's buttons strained further as he bent forward to make sure he had heard correctly.

"No, she is keeping to her rooms."

"Oh." He was clearly disappointed.

Molly sat on one of the two red settees that faced each other in front of the white marble fireplace. She saw the earl looking impatiently toward the door and suspected he was waiting for his brother.

Just then, Henry dashed in, mumbling apologies for being late and rattling the gold chain on his watch fob as noisily as if it were steel links. He wore a bright yellow coat and a cravat tied in dizzying intricacies. He cast smiles around the room. "Everything looks right as a trivet now that the furniture is back. Mother must be excessively pleased. Where is she?"

"Resting." The earl cleared his throat. "It is time to go in to dinner."

Henry offered his arm to Antonia, who beamed up at him.

The earl came forward and gave his arm to Molly. She was not used to such formality, especially in a small group, but they were in England now, she reminded herself. Even in Ireland, some families stood on ceremony. Her parents had not raised Molly and her two sisters with an undue emphasis on protocol, although Molly had been taught how to conduct herself under more formal circumstances. It looked as if this was going to be one of those circumstances, she thought as they marched into the dining room. They were seated around a long, doubt-pedestal table that had sat in Kindred Manor only a few days ago. A servant stood behind every Queen Anne chair. More servants in dignified dark blue livery whisked in and out carrying steaming dishes.

"I trust your trip was pleasant," the earl said courteously to Sir Brace.

"Quite."

Molly looked over at her uncle and was glad to note the smell of fine food seemed to overcome his disappointment about Lady Lindworth's absence.

"The young ladies were able to see Icknield Way," her uncle continued. "You know it, don't you? It's a footpath where the ruts from Roman chariot wheels are still etched in the chalk."

The earl nodded politely. "That must have been interesting."

Lord Lindworth was making an effort to be pleasant, Molly conceded. Still, she was glad they would leave soon. They planned to make a leisurely return trip back, stopping in London. Molly was already trying to decide what present she would buy to take back to Daniel in Ireland.

"This is a splendid house," Sir Brace said. "I like a structure that is old and enduring and has seen a bit of history."

"A deal of history," Henry agreed affably. "Many ghosts walk these halls."

Antonia looked up, her fork hanging in midair, her eyes wide. "Do you ever see ghosts in the passageways?"

"What? Oh, no, that is just a manner of speaking. The house is not haunted." Henry laughed heartily at the thought.

The earl glanced toward Antonia as if noticing her for the first time. She looked pretty and prim in a forest green dress with a little ivory satin ruff around the neck. Molly waited. If he was rude to Antonia or made her feel unwelcome at the table, Molly would stab him with her butter knife. But he nodded pleasantly toward the girl.

At Sir Brace's prompting, the earl explained some of the history of the house and about how various ancestors had added on to the original house until they had built a square that enclosed a courtyard in the center. Henry bored of such conversation quickly and turned the talk to horses. He had to stop now and again to explain that a rattler and prads was a coach and horses and that bo-kickers were horses that were hard to handle.

Sir Brace spoke about the trip over from Ireland and the rough seas. At the mention of the voyage, Molly sank in her chair. She had been seasick during the whole trip. She dreaded crossing the Irish Sea to return home.

Lord Lindworth noticed her reaction. "Was it an unpleasant journey, Miss Mills?"

" 'Twas dreadful."

"Lawrence can well understand that," Henry put in energetically. "He got sick as a drunken ostler when he crossed the Channel. Didn't you, Lawrence? He was hanging over the side, face green as one of your Irish shamrocks and—"

66

"Henry . . ." The earl gave him a quelling look.

The younger man glanced at the ladies, reddened, and apologized.

Molly sympathized with Lord Lindworth's seasickness. She had endured the same agony. "I hope the return trip will not be so bad," she said.

"You are going back to Ireland?" Henry asked.

"As soon as possible."

"Can't imagine why. There is no city in all of Ireland to rival London. No entertainments of consequence. Must be boring."

"Dublin is a grand city," Molly informed him pertly. "There is also a great deal of culture in Ireland. If it had not been for Irish monks keeping learning alive when it had been all but abandoned in England, people here in your country would be living like savages."

"My niece knows a great deal about Irish history," Sir Brace reported proudly.

"If the monks were so bang up to the mark, why did they live in poverty?" Henry retorted. He had dripped some wine onto his cravat. The red stain widened as he wiped carelessly at it. Across from him, a servant watched in horror.

"Because they chose to," she said loftily.

"Dashed shatterbrained of them, if you ask me."

Molly looked at Henry. He was young and rich and without a thought in his head except horses. Still, there was something affable about him, and she could not judge him too harshly. At least he had a pleasing humor that was missing in his brother. "I shall tell them you said they were shatterbrained when I return home." She could not repress a smile.

"My niece is in no hurry to go back," Sir Brace

put in. "She may come to like England so well, she decides to stay here forever."

Molly knew that would never happen.

Near the door leading in from the kitchen, there was a flurry of activity, and a small herd of servants entered carrying silver tureens and platters of eels en matelote.

"What do you think happened to the gypsy man who took your belongings?" Sir Brace asked over the onslaught of rattling dishes.

"I do not yet know, but I have hired a gentleman named Mr. Miller to find him."

Molly glanced at the earl. "What difference will it be making now?" she asked. "You have recovered everything that was taken."

"At great inconvenience," Lord Lindworth snapped.

Sir Brace interjected quickly, "Has your man Miller had any luck finding the gypsy?"

"Not yet, but he has spoken with several people who saw the band of gypsies camped outside of Kent. I should not be surprised if Mr. Miller does not overtake them soon."

"How can one man confront a band of gypsies?" Molly thought the earl was not only stubborn, he was foolish. Mr. Miller was even more foolish if he was willing to accuse a gang of unruly gypsies of anything.

"He will contact the authorities," the earl told her frostily.

"I see." She turned her attention back to her plate. The food was splendid even if the company was not.

"So the prince will arrive soon?" Sir Brace made another hearty effort at changing the conversation.

"Yes."

"That must be very exciting."

Antonia looked up. "Is he married?"

"Yes," Lord Lindworth said.

"Will his wife come with him?"

The earl cleared his throat uncomfortably. "I do not think so."

"He travels alone?" Antonia asked sympathetically. "How sad for him."

"He has companions," the earl assured the young girl.

Molly was pleased that the earl was pleasant to her cousin. It seemed to be his one redeeming trait.

"Female ones," Henry contributed between bites of tartlets. "Mrs. Fitzherbert, of course, is no longer his light-o-lo—"

"Henry, do you find the watercress to your liking?" the earl asked. Lest Henry fail to understand, Lord Lindworth glanced pointedly toward Antonia.

"Mrs. Fitzherbert. That sounds like an Irish name," Antonia said. "Is she a particular friend of the prince's?"

"Well, yes, she was," the earl said in a strangled voice.

"I know several Fitzherberts near Galway. She might know them."

"I doubt it is the same family," Lord Lindworth said.

Molly reflected the earl would surely be more universally liked if he treated everyone with the same respectful kindness he showed Antonia.

The rest of the meal passed without incident, and Molly and Antonia went upstairs afterward to Molly's room.

"Papa seems happy to be here." Antonia sat on the floor near Molly's bed, a candle beside her as she practiced drawing elaborate calligraphy Xs on a sheet of parchment. "Do you think spending a night or two in Lord Lindworth's residence will change people's minds about Papa? Do you think he will then be included in society?"

Molly sighed. "I do not think so." If their hostess did not even greet them or join them for dinner, it did not bode well for Sir Brace.

"I like Lord Lindworth now that I know him better." Antonia pulled at the ruff around her neck.

Molly said nothing. Once Antonia was old enough to have better judgment about men, she would realize the earl was stiff beyond bearing.

"I think you have misjudged him," Antonia continued. "He is like a hero from a Mrs. Radcliffe novel. He seems cold and forbidding at first, but upon further acquaintance, he is charming."

"Humph."

"Really," Antonia insisted.

Molly looked down into her cousin's upturned face and realized the child had developed a girlish affection for the dreadful earl. Antonia's last *tendre* had been for a stable hand who put down bowls of milk for stray cats. Antonia had taken a great interest in riding her little mare for several weeks and was constantly at the stables seeing to her bridle and horse and adding milk to the bowls. In the end, the man had broken her heart by marrying a pretty maid from the village.

Thank goodness Molly and Antonia would only be around the earl another day or so. Then they could go home and forget he existed.

* * *

Early the next morning Lord Lindworth prepared or his ride. He enjoyed riding while the dew was till on the grass, and his horse, Hecate, was restess after a night in the stables. Upon his return, e planned to work on his architectural sketches. t was too bad he would have to interrupt his work t midmorning to entertain guests, but there was o other solution since he had received a message rom his mother last night that she intended to keep o her rooms all day. She had clearly decided to andle the indelicate matter of Sir Brace's visit by voiding her visitors.

The pink of dawn was still in the sky when the earl walked out the back door and crossed the cobblestoned drive to the stables. His groom stood holding the dancing stallion.

"Good morning, Jim. Hecate looks ready to go."

"Yes, sir." The groom hesitated, then added, "A lady guest was here a moment ago and asked me to saddle a gentle horse for riding. I thought Saisons might be a good mount for her."

"A lady?" Lord Lindworth repeated. No ladies of his acquaintance were ever up at this hour.

"Yes, sir. Red of hair and rather comely of form, if you take my meaning." He winked broadly.

The earl did indeed take his meaning. Jim could only mean Miss Mills, with her full woman's breasts, narrow waist, and slender hips.

"Where is the lady now?" the earl asked.

"I told her it would take a moment to prepare a mount, and she went bounding off into the pasture." He looked over the earl's shoulder. "She is returning now."

As Lord Lindworth turned, he saw her coming toward him. Her cheeks were as pink as the dawn

71

sky, and her eyes as green as the wet grass catch
ing at her long blue skirts. A small bonnet with
long blue plume sat daintily atop her head. Besid
her bounded a large red dog. The earl recalled see
ing the dog yesterday while the men were unload
ing the carts. They must have brought the anima
with them from Bath.

"Good morning, Miss Mills. I understand yo
wish to ride. I am just getting ready to go for m
own ride and would deem it a pleasure if you joine
me." He had worked late last night and had mad
good progress designing a series of arches to sepa
rate one London street from another. He was i
good humor and feeling particularly charitable.

She smiled but shook her head. "The dog is rest
less. I shall walk him some more instead of riding.'

"As you wish." He took the reins from his groom
mounted, and galloped off across the meadow.

As a rule, Lawrence enjoyed his solitary rides. I
gave him the opportunity to watch deer and dor
mice and to smell the wildflowers that burst across
the meadows in the late summer. In the spring,
bluebells ran riot over the forest floor before the
canopy of beech leaves shooed them away. Just now,
with fall approaching, the acorns hung green and
heavy on the trees, and tiny yellow flowers danced
around in the meadows.

Today, however, he was not of a mind to appreciate
the beauty of his surroundings. Miss Mills had a right
to decline his offer to ride with him. The dog had not
seemed at all restless to him, but if she said that it
needed to be walked, who was he to question her?
Never mind that half the women in London would
vie for the opportunity to ride alongside him. If Miss
Mills did not wish to, that was her choice.

A short time later, Hecate trotted back up to the stable door and came to a meek if perplexed halt. She whinnied over her shoulder as if asking why they had returned so soon. Lord Lindworth slid down off his mount and shouted for Jim.

The servant appeared and took the horse.

"Your lady guest went for a ride."

The earl stared at him. "What did you say?"

"Not long after you left, she took Saisons out. Begging your pardon, sir, but it appeared that she waited until you were out of sight before leaving. She has little skill as a horsewoman," he added.

The earl was not interested in Miss Mills's prowess with horses. What the devil did the chit mean refusing to ride with him and then going off alone?

"Did she have a companion or chaperon?"

"No."

"I see." Lord Lindworth marched back toward the house. To ride out without an escort was beyond countenancing, especially after she had declined to go with him. Well, what did he expect from an Irishwoman?

He strode into the house, passing a startled maid without a glance. Once in his study, he settled himself into the big chair behind his desk, spread out his drawings, and forced his attention to his work. It took concentration, but he finally made himself forget Miss Molly Mills.

Should the area around Carlton House that the prince wished to rebuild reflect the classical mood of the country or should it contain some of the earlier Gothic elements? Should it be large and ornate or small and discreet? White marble or local stone?

A servant appeared sometime in the afternoon with a tray of food, and Lawrence absently ate as he continued refining his plans. Beside him, working quietly at a desk and concentrating as determinedly as Lord Lindworth, sat his secretary, Webber Kindley.

Lawrence was absorbed in his work when Henry appeared in the middle of the afternoon. Henry wore leather breeches and a striped coat and had a quiver of arrows slung over his shoulder. "Sir Brace's daughter is worried. I was practicing my archery and had just landed an arrow dead in the center of the target when she found me. It was my best shot of the day. Well, I had a better one this morning, but it was with a wooden arrow and not with—"

"What did the girl want, Henry?"

"Oh. She is concerned about her cousin. Says she has not seen Miss Mills since last night."

"Miss Mills went for a ride this morning. Alone," Lord Lindworth said tersely.

"Jim told me that, but she has not returned."

The earl looked up, pulled out his watch, and frowned. She had been gone far too long for any simple ride. Something must be wrong.

"The young girl feared a ghost or some evil person might have seized Miss Mills," Henry reported with a smirk.

Lawrence was already rising. "I do not believe in ghosts, but I believe in accidents." She might have been tossed from her horse and injured. Or she could be lost, circling futilely in the deep forests or tramping through the meadows without any idea how to get back to the house. At any rate, her failure to return was cause for alarm.

"Order a pair of horses saddled," Lord Lindworth commanded. "You and I shall go look. Have one saddled for Sir Brace."

"He cannot join us," Henry said. "He is unwell and has taken to his bed."

"Then we will have some of the stable hands help." The earl started toward the door. As his heavy boots sounded on the polished hallway, he silently upbraided Miss Mills for riding out alone in an unfamiliar place. Any Englishwoman would have known better.

The five men who galloped away from the stables a short time later each took a separate road or path leading from the house. Lord Lindworth searched the glen near the stream that rushed along the outer edge of the property. With each hour he spent poking at bushes with his whip and sliding from his horse to check for fresh tracks, his concern grew.

The hours crept on. The blue of the sky turned pearl gray as daylight waned. Beneath the trees, the shadows grew longer and more menacing. More serious fears presented themselves. What if she was seriously injured? What if someone had accosted her? Highwaymen were infrequent, but they did exist. A lone woman with a pretty figure and compelling green eyes might be prey to someone with a baser desire than robbery. Blast the woman. Why had she ridden off alone?

Lawrence was canvassing the road that led to an ancient stone circle when he heard a shout. He reined in his horse and scanned the rolling hills. With darkness almost upon him, it was difficult to tell the rocks and trees from the form of a person. Then he saw a movement and peered hard. It was Miss Mills scrambling down a hill toward him.

Her hair streamed out behind her, and she carried her bonnet dangling from its ribbons.

Was she hurt? No, she did not appear injured, he

noted with relief. Having ascertained that she was safe, his anger struck like a hammer hitting metal. He slid off his horse and stalked toward her. "I trust you can explain your actions, Miss Mills. You have caused—" He ground to a halt as he reached her. Her face and hands were badly scratched. An ugly purplish gash slashed above her right eye. Even more arresting than her injuries was her relief as she gazed up at him. The green eyes were alight with gratitude.

She stretched a hand eagerly toward him. "Thank goodness you are here."

He held himself taut. "What happened?"

"The horse tossed me into the briars and ran away." She gestured feebly. "Hours ago it was. I tried to walk back to the house through the woods. I thought it would be shorter than following the road, but I got lost and wandered for such a long time. I found a stream and followed it here, but it was already growing dark and I had no idea where I was." Her voice trembled as she added, "I had begun to fear I would have to spend the night here alone."

He did not unbend even though she looked small and frightened. She should not have gone off by herself. Her cousin and uncle were probably at wits' end, and several good men had wasted time searching for her. "You have caused a great deal of worry."

"I am sorry, but it could not be helped. The horse threw me."

"Of course it could have been helped," he snapped. She had acted in a headstrong and careless manner. "I invited you to join me in a ride this morning. Had you gone with me, as any sensible woman would have done, this would not have happened."

She blinked as if she had been slapped. Then she

stepped back from him and drew herself up rigidly. "You asked me to join you because you felt obliged to and not because you had any desire for my company."

"I did not say that."

"No, but it was perfectly obvious. You did not invite my uncle and myself here, and you did not wish us to come. I saw no reason to further inflict myself upon you."

He scowled at her. He would not have looked upon a ride with a beautiful woman as a thoroughly disagreeable task, but it was ridiculous to stand here and argue with the chit while darkness engulfed them. He could not change events. What he ought to do was return her to the house with all due speed, deposit her in the bosom of her family, and wash his hands of her.

Lord Lindworth drew a long breath and said in a carefully neutral voice, "I think we should return to Wicklowe Hall."

Molly looked toward his horse. "How? You only have one mount."

It was true. In his haste to begin the search for her, he had not considered that. He could go back to the stables and get another horse, but it would be difficult to find her again in the darkness. Besides, he did not think she would accept being left here alone on a dark road. That left only one solution. "You must ride behind me," he said curtly.

Molly hesitated.

His patience ebbed. "Unless you prefer to wait here while I return to the house and get another horse for you?"

"I am already cold and tired," she said crossly. "I've no wish to be left by myself in the dark." She looked toward the horse, sighed, then started wordlessly toward it.

Lord Lindworth followed. In silence he put his hands together to form a step to help her up into the saddle. She scrambled up onto the horse and sat looking woefully down at him. "I do not like horses, especially large ones. Please mount quickly before this one bolts and kills me."

"Hecate is not going to bolt." He swung himself up to sit in front of Miss Mills. There was not a lot of room on a horse, even a big horse, he realized as he felt Miss Mills's body fitted close to his. She felt chilled and small. He resolved not to notice.

"Put your arms around my waist," he commanded. "Tightly."

She obeyed and they started back to the house. Of course, he knew this violated every rule of decorum. A gentleman and lady should not ride in such a fashion, but they must get back to the house, and this was the only sensible means of accomplishing that. Still, he would be glad enough when they reached the house and she was dispatched to her room. The earl had endured enough of Miss Mills for the day. He wished she had not gone for a ride by herself, and he wished her warm breath were not tickling against his ear in such an unsettling fashion.

He steeled himself to keep from softening at the memory of her bedraggled and vulnerable appearance. She had looked at him with such gratitude that he was sorry he had shouted at her. Then he reminded himself he could not afford such thoughts concerning her.

Chapter 5

MOLLY SAT in her bed with a cup of hot tea beside her. A soft green peignoir lay over her shoulders, and the ribbons that tied it together floated down over her chemise.

Antonia, who was seated on the floor, leaned forward eagerly. "Then what happened? Did he attempt to kiss you?"

"Do not be absurd, Antonia. We came back to the house, and there is an end to it."

"You were lost all day. This is just like a heroine from a novel. And you were rescued by the dashing, heroic earl. How romantic."

Molly pursed her lips. "Not long ago you were picturing Lord Lindworth as a villain."

"Yes, but he is far too handsome for that. I cannot see him shuffling about the dark passageways in the middle of the night. Really he would have to have a dragging limp or a hump on his back for that. I have decided he would make a better hero."

"It was anything but romantic," Molly grumbled.

"To be whisked up onto the earl's horse and carried back to safety sounds grand and wonderful," Antonia said dreamily. "Are you certain he did not kiss you?"

Molly did not dignify that impertinent question with a reply.

"Do the scratches hurt?" Antonia asked on a more down-to-earth note.

"No." Molly had been back less than an hour. She and the earl had arrived at the house to be greeted in the front hallway by Antonia and a group of anxious servants. After assuring everyone she was unharmed, Molly had retired to her room, bathed her wounds, changed into a light gown, and taken to her bed. There she had had time to reflect on Lord Lindworth's brusqueness toward her and to nurse her resentment toward him. Yes, she had acted unwisely to ride out by herself, but his scolding still rankled.

"It was kind of the earl to invite us to delay our departure until you are well enough to travel."

"We shall leave tomorrow," Molly asserted. "I only need a night's rest to recover." She was more than ready to leave Lord Lindworth's haughty presence. He had not spoken one word to her throughout the ride back. He had not even asked if the scratches hurt. Arrogant Englishman.

"Oh, we cannot leave tomorrow. Papa's gout has returned."

Molly frowned. Uncle Brace had not been in the hall with the others when she returned, but in the excitement she had scarcely noticed. "His gout did not bother him on the trip up from Bath." He had taken care not to eat rich foods or imbibe in strong drink. How strange that he was suddenly so ill he could not leave his room.

Antonia shrugged and turned to a subject of greater interest. "I have explored the library and discovered some excellent old manuscripts."

"Did you ask permission before going into the library?" They had already offended the earl enough; Molly did not wish to hear another lecture from the earl tomorrow.

"There was no one to ask. Lord Lindworth and Henry were out looking for you, and Lady Lindworth kept to her rooms." Antonia leaned farther forward to ask in a whisper, "Do you think she is avoiding us?"

"Yes." Which was all the more reason they must quit this house tomorrow. That is, if Uncle Brace was better.

"Maybe she is being held a prisoner," Antonia suggested urgently. "She might be locked in a dark room somewhere with little to eat and a horrid woman guarding her. What if we are to be the next victims—"

"To bed with you then, Antonia, before you make yourself too frightened to venture down the halls."

"It is possible she is a prisoner."

"No, it is not."

Sighing at Molly's lack of imagination, Antonia rose, gave her a kiss, and left.

Molly blew out the candle beside her bed and lay inhaling the scent of the hot wax. Lord Lindworth's mother was not a prisoner; it was far more likely she was unsufferably arrogant and would not deign to meet them. As to Antonia's question of the earl kissing Molly, that did not even bear thinking about.

Yet she did think about it anyway. Men and women who shared kisses must harbor strong emotions toward each other. The idea of she and the earl sharing anything but polite dislike of each other escaped Molly. Even if he was handsome and possessed of a pair of fine gray eyes, he was not the sort she would kiss.

Molly's last thought before she fell sleep was to hope Uncle Brace was better on the morrow so they could be gone and she could forget all about the earl.

"Hartshorn, Lawrence. I am going to swoon again."

"Mother, it is only for one more day. We cannot toss them out if the man is ill."

"They *have* to leave." Lady Lindworth regarded her son earnestly. She looked very tiny sitting in a massive black chair with lion heads carved into the arms. The earl and his mother were in the large room at the back of the house that had once served the monks as a sleeping chamber. Lawrence had chosen it for his study and work room because of the good light that came in through the bank of multifoiled windows that arched together to form scalloped edges at the sides and a grand five-leafed pane at the top.

"You must understand, Lawrence. Every day they remain hurts us. We cannot welcome into our home a man the king ordered out of the country!"

"It will only be one more day," Lawrence repeated gently. He had no more wish to entertain their guests than did his mother. He had his own business to attend to. He had lost precious time yesterday looking for Molly Mills. He had lost more time last night in his bed when he should have been sleeping but instead recalled the shape of her body against his and the wild honeysuckle scent that clung to her hair.

Rising, Lady Lindworth flitted about the room.

n her expensive gray gown, she looked like an anxious gray bird. "How do we know that? They must be gone by the time the prince arrives. They simply must!"

"That is above a week from now, Mother."

"Who is to say Sir Brace's illness will not linger? One can never predict sickness."

She was right on that head. People afflicted with gout sometimes suffered for weeks at a time. Even months. Lawrence pushed that unwelcome thought aside.

His mother continued to move restlessly about the room. "We could have Sir Brace bled. That ought to cure him. It always cured Lord Willoughby's gout."

"Lord Willoughby is dead," the earl reminded her.

"Well, he is no longer suffering from gout," she said stoutly. Then, as if the rare display of spirit had drained her, Lady Lindworth subsided back into the large chair and wrung her hands. The heavy jewels in her rings scraped against one another. "This is by everything dreadful." She looked tearfully up at him. "But I know you will manage everything. You are so good at such things."

Lawrence was silent. When his father was alive, his mother had relied on him to attend to unpleasant matters. Now such tasks fell to her oldest son. As earl, of course, it was his duty to oversee family concerns. Just now, however, he was tired, irritable, and in no humor to contemplate how best to rid his household of undesirable guests.

"Lady Selwith is having a ball tomorrow night. I should like to attend, but if I do, everyone will quiz me about the guests. Our servants have talked, you know, and everyone knows they are here." She looked at him helplessly. "What am I to do?"

"We shall deal with that tomorrow, Mother." Lawrence ran a hand through his short, black hair and thought of all the unfinished work on his desk. "This may all solve itself and Sir Brace may feel splendid when he awakens."

Somehow Lawrence did not think the problem was going to go away that easily. While Sir Brace might be the cause of their dilemma, his niece remained the person in Lord Lindworth's thoughts. What Miss Mills needed was someone to take a firm hand with her. He would not relish the task. She was far too headstrong and spirited to ever make a proper lady.

Still, those sparking green eyes and soft pink cheeks might entice an unwary man. It was fortunate he was far too wise to become embroiled with someone like her. Not that he would ever consider anyone like her for a bride, but a man could not help pondering what pretty charms lay waiting for discovery.

He caught the direction his thoughts were taking, drew himself upright, and returned to his desk to work.

Molly tapped on her uncle's door and pushed it open. The door swung on well-oiled hinges, making only the slightest noise. Sir Brace looked up from the corner of the large room where he sat near a fireplace of softly glowing black marble. His foot was propped on cushions on a small stool in front of him, and a book lay open in his lap.

Uncle Brace's color, Molly was glad to see, was

good. There were no lines of fatigue or pain around his eyes.

"Are you feeling better?" she asked cheerfully.

He closed the book and looked at her mournfully. "I am in great pain."

He did not appear so. She supposed one could not always tell by looking. "I am sorry to hear that. Do you think we ought to ask a doctor to come look at your foot?"

"No." He looked toward the window that opened out onto a courtyard enveloped on all sides by the house.

"A doctor might be able to help," she said.

"Butchers, all of them! They'd as lief take off your leg as try to heal something as simple as a scratch."

She was surprised to find her uncle so intractable. He must be suffering more than she had imagined.

He looked at her more fully and frowned. "What is that on your face?"

Molly touched the cut above her eye. "Nothing. I am far more concerned about you. Would you like me to look at your foot?" She moved toward him and bent to lift the light cover from his foot. "I might be able to bandage it or—"

"Don't touch it!"

Molly backed away. She had never seen him so adamant. "I only want to help."

Softening immediately, he smiled at her. "I know you do, but you must not concern yourself about me. You ought to amuse yourself. You and Antonia could go see the countryside or shop in the village for silver. Or find a good mount in the stables and go for a ride."

Molly had gone for a ride yesterday, much to her regret.

"Are you and Lord Lindworth becoming friends?" he asked with hope in his voice.

"Of course not. He is a stiff-necked Englishman, and we could never be friends."

"Pity. Well, Henry seems an agreeable sort."

"Yes." Henry was not so constrained by the rules that made his brother so unyielding and rigid.

Her uncle yawned.

Molly started guiltily for the door. "You are tired. I'll be letting you rest then." She pulled the door closed behind her and went in search of Antonia.

Her cousin was not in her room, nor in any of the rooms on the ground level that Molly searched. She finally wandered through an open door into a big room with a row of pretty windows along one wall. She saw Lord Lindworth standing in front of a table cluttered with papers. A man sitting at another table appeared to be drawing something.

"I am sorry to disturb you; I was looking for my cousin."

"She has gone into town with Henry," Lord Lindworth said.

"Oh? I did not know Antonia had plans to go into town."

"You need not fear. Her maid went along, so it is perfectly proper."

"That was not my concern," she said crisply. He might spend all his time worrying about propriety, but she did not. "I thought she and I might go somewhere together."

"Your cousin found herself in sudden, urgent need for books which my library does not possess." A smile overtook him, and he shrugged. "We have only volumes of literature. She needed something with blood and castle spires and secret passages. I was given to understand a ghost or two would be welcome."

Molly's own lips curved into a smile. "She does like her gothic romances."

"Yes." Lord Lindworth put his drawings aside and came around the table toward her. "Are you bored, Miss Mills?"

"I have nothing of a particular nature to do," she confessed. She could have worked on the manuscript she was copying for the church in Galway, but it was a sunny day and she wanted to go out and feel the breeze and smell the air.

His smile deepened. She had not realized his smile could be so warm and sincere. "Perhaps you are also in need of something to read. I shall be glad to take you to the lending library."

Molly saw no reason to demur for politeness' sake. She welcomed the chance to go somewhere, even with the earl. "I would like that."

"I shall have the carriage sent round and meet you in the front hall in fifteen minutes. Will that give you time to fetch your pelisse?"

What a silly question. Her pelisse was a small pink garment, not some heavy burden whose weight would slow her as she trudged through the halls to the front hall.

"That will be sufficient time, milord."

Molly reached the front door fifteen minutes later just as the earl arrived. She had not noticed his clothes before, but now she saw he wore brown breeches and a jade green jacket, and carried an ebony walking stick. For sartorial splendor alone,

one could find no objections, Molly reflected as she pulled her delicate pelisse around her shoulders.

He raised one dark slash of an eyebrow in approval. "You are very punctual. I thought I would have to wait. I almost always find myself waiting for ladies."

Molly sniffed. "It's little patience I have with people who are late. You should drive off and leave them."

"One does not do such things in England." He held the heavy front door for her, and she stepped past him headed toward his sporty tilbury.

She gave a saucy toss of her head. "Oh, I had quite forgotten we are in England. Naturally you could not do such a thing in a refined country such as this. In Ireland, on the other hand, we throw people who are late into the ocean and beat them back when they try to climb out." She halted beside the tilbury and blinked up at him with innocent eyes. "Do you think we deal too harshly with them?"

"Not as harshly as you do with me," he muttered as he handed her up.

"I am persuaded you are able to hold your own, milord," she said, and immediately regretted her tartness. She did not intend to cross swords with him. He had spent time looking for her yesterday, and today he was taking her into town. She intended to make herself agreeable.

He picked up the reins and they started down the elm-lined drive. He handled the high-spirited bays well, she noted. She respected anyone adept at handling horses. Her own skills were not good, as yesterday's misadventure proved.

"Is the village old?" she asked pleasantly.

"It dates from the ninth century."

"Really? How grand." She politely did not contradict him even though the guidebook had said it was built in the fifteenth century, although there was a ruined chancel from much earlier. "Do you spend most of your time here or in London?"

"In London. I only came to Wicklowe Hall to prepare for the prince's visit."

"You looked busy in your study. Is that in anticipation of His Majesty's visit?"

"Yes, I am drawing up architectural plans for some changes to London." He seemed relaxed, handling the reins with ease and occasionally glancing at her as he spoke. To anyone passing, they might have appeared a friendly couple out taking the air. Who would know she was an unwanted guest?

They fell into conversation about inconsequential matters.

She was enjoying the ride when he asked, "Would you prefer to go to the lending library first, or do you wish to stop at the emporium for some bits of lace?"

Glancing up, she realized they had entered the town. It was a quaint little village of stucco and brick with signs hanging above doorways to identify the White Stag Inn and the Wayfarer's Tavern. Lord Lindworth reined in the horses behind a slow-moving cart.

"The library," she said. The town lay on the edge of a slope that looked out over beech groves and square pastures of various shades of green. The long, straight street that led into town was flanked by apothecary and glover's shops.

He pulled the tilbury into the inn courtyard, helped her down, and escorted her a block away to the lending library. She entered a room with high ceilings and cool air. Rows of bookshelves lined the walls and marched down the center of the room. Several customers milled about. Molly spied Henry standing against a wall holding an armload of books and tapping his foot impatiently.

"Do you think a book about witches would be more diverting than one about an ancient curse?" Antonia asked Henry. Her face was tilted up toward the top row of a shelf as she examined titles. Her arms were also laden with books.

"Either would be equally revolting," Henry said with worldly ennui. "This is what comes of living too long in Ireland. Young ladies in England do not fill their heads with such nonsense."

"They must lead very dull lives," Antonia snipped. She turned and saw Molly and broke into a smile. "I am sorry I came away without you, but Henry offered to bring me into town, and I could not find you. He is going to teach me to shoot a bow when we return to the house," she added.

"That is very kind of him." Molly thought Henry must be bored with his enforced stay in the country and willing to do almost anything for diversion. She suspected his interest ran more to horse racing and gaming than it did to entertaining a young girl. Yet he was trapped at Wicklowe Hall until after the prince's visit.

While Antonia continued selecting gothic stories, Molly started down the nearest aisle. The earl followed. As she scanned the bulging shelves, she thought of how precious few were the books the Irish monks had owned all those centuries ago. "So many books," she murmured as she rounded a corner.

"Indeed there are," a man agreed, and smiled first at her, then at the earl. "Your companion has a charming accent, Lawrence."

Molly looked up into the approving eyes of a tall, blond man. A gap between his front teeth kept him from being entirely handsome, but he had a broad, likable smile. Any man who looked at her with such utter fascination could not be bad, she decided.

"She is from Ireland, Alfred." The earl, clearly seeing no way to avoid introductions, stiffly introduced Molly to the Marquis of Norton.

Lord Norton bowed low over Molly's hand. "England is the richer for your presence." His gaze never left her face as he said over her hand to Lord Lindworth, "You have been unkind to keep such a beauty to yourself. You must bring her to see my mother and sisters. I know they would be delighted."

"Miss Mills will be leaving soon."

Lord Norton looked reproachfully at the earl. "Surely not before the prince arrives." To Molly he said, "You must not let Lawrence be so unchivalrous as to allow you to go without meeting Prinny. Really, Lawrence, I am shocked at you."

Molly glanced archly over her shoulder to see how her host received the setdown.

"I am afraid we cannot linger to talk." Lord Lindworth impassively took her arm and guided her toward the door. "Miss Mills and I have several other shops she wishes to visit. Good day, Alfred."

On the sidewalk outside the bookstore, she looked sweetly up at him. "What other shops?"

"We shall buy some chocolate at Brendram's. They serve ices that are almost as nice as Gunther's."

Molly blinked earnestly. "But if you take me into a shop, another acquaintance might see you, and you would be forced to introduce me again. Sooner or later—" she dropped her voice to a breathless whisper and made her eyes wide "—someone is going to discover who my uncle is, and you will have no choice but to run yourself through with your sword." She glanced toward his hip. "Dear me, I see you are not wearing your sword today."

He glared at her, the steel gray eyes snapping. "Are you quite through, Miss Mills?"

"For the moment," she said with an innocent smile. Her words had contained home truths, and she knew he disliked her all the more for that. No one had ever been ashamed of her before, and she resented being treated as an inconvenience now.

"Then I suggest we have an ice. By the time we are through, your cousin should have selected enough books to raise the hair on her scalp for several days."

"I have no appetite for an ice," she countered pertly. "I believe I shall go into this shop and see what goods they are selling." She sailed into the emporium without a backward glance at him. Let him wait, she decided as she wandered about touching pretty calico fabrics, examining a length of Belgium lace, and debating over fringe for a new bonnet. Waiting would not even be a just punishment for his arrogance.

The earl stood in the corner, looking completely elegant in his fine clothes and glowering darkly. She did not hurry. He *had* offered to bring her to town, and she smarted from his reluctance to introduce her to his friend. As her fingers brushed over the smooth satins and crisp frills of lace, her thoughts turned to her uncle. What could he have done to make his family so undesirable that she could not even be introduced? Had he murdered someone? Compromised an unprotected woman? What?

The time had come to learn the truth, Molly decided.

Leaving a disappointed shopkeeper hovering near the door, Molly crossed the street and allowed the earl to hand her into the tilbury. Once they were on their way out of town, she turned to him and asked forthrightly, "What did my uncle do to make him so unacceptable in his own country?"

Lord Lindworth did not look at her. "You should ask Sir Brace."

"I have asked him, but the question upsets him."

They rode in silence.

"I am waiting," she said.

His aristocratic jaw tightened. "If you must know, your uncle hit King George the Third."

Molly waited for more. "That is all?"

"Yes."

For that the family was excluded from Bath society thirty years later? "The king is so mad, he cannot even rule his own country. His son had to be named regent to rule in his stead. What difference does it make what arguments the king had in the past?"

Lord Lindworth stiffened. "The fight with your uncle was long before his madness."

She waved her hand dismissingly. "Men fight all the time. Some even go to boxing salons and pay to hit each other—if you can imagine anything so ridiculous."

"If you are referring to Gentleman Jackson's, I frequent it myself," he informed her curtly.

"There, you see. Even men who are supposed to have breeding hit each other."

"In acceptable places and following carefully laid-out rules. No one of my acquaintance would ever behave as improperly as your uncle did."

From behind them came the sound of rushing hooves. They both turned to look at the high-perch phaeton bringing up rapidly behind them. Henry and Antonia sat inside. Antonia was driving. They careened by, with Antonia waving gaily as she passed.

Molly called a greeting.

The earl scowled.

She turned back to him. "You were saying that my uncle behaved improperly. What difference does it make after all these years?" It did not matter to her how society viewed her beloved uncle, but since it was important to Uncle Brace to be readmitted into society, she must at least try to make Lord Lindworth see reason.

"It matters because things are done a certain way in polite society," he said coldly.

"Then they are done wrong. It is foolish to behave as if hitting a king is the same as killing someone. It is not. Besides, Uncle Brace has served his punishment by living out of the country all these years. Now he wishes to return, and people should be generous enough to accept him back."

"We take our responsibility to royalty seriously," the earl said piously.

"Pooh!"

Having delivered herself of this opinion, Molly turned to face the road. Neither she nor the earl spoke to each other the remainder of the trip. She could feel his cold disapproval, and she was sure he recognized her impatience.

Lord Lindworth returned from town in a bad temper. He had taken Miss Mills into town as a gesture of kindness. Instead of appreciating his efforts, she had arrived back at the house with her chin tilted up defiantly. He had dealt with women since his salad days, and he was well practiced at handling headstrong chits. But Miss Mills recognized neither his wisdom nor his position, and she refused to bow to either.

To make matters worse, when he returned to his study, his secretary, Webber Kindley, sat by the window with his head in his hands. Lawrence saw at a glance that Webber's skin was sallow and his eyes watery.

"Are you sick?" The question sounded sharper than Lawrence intended. It was not to his credit that his first thought was how inconvenient it would be if Webber fell ill when there was so much to be done.

"I am flushed and chilled by turns, and my head hurts."

Webber Kindley's father had been in the employ of Lawrence's family since before either boy was born. Webber had been educated by the same tutors as Lawrence. It was Webber who meticulously redrew the sketches of buildings the earl made in rough draft. Webber was tall and spare and somber of appearance. Usually he was hale and healthy; just now, however, he looked as if he might collapse at any moment onto the multihued Oriental rug.

Well, there was nothing for it, Lawrence thought wearily. "You must go to bed."

"I cannot. There is too much to do."

"You are not able to work."

"There is no one else."

That was true. Lawrence looked at the piles of work on the table and briefly considered pressing Henry into service. Then he recalled his brother's indifferent penmanship and wandering attention. The earl did not wish to present an ink-blotted mess to the prince. "I shall do it myself. To bed with you."

Webbed lacked the strength to argue. "Thank you, milord." He rose and dragged himself out of the room. Lord Lindworth watched him go, then looked back at the work. Sighing, he crossed to the desk and sat down. He would be up late tonight and every night for the next week. It was a pity he did not know anyone else who possessed the ability to draw well.

"Henry let me handle the reins all the way back from town," Antonia bragged as she sat on Molly's bed drawing on a piece of paper and scratching an insect bite on her neck. It was late evening, and the two had just returned from dinner.

"Did he then?" Molly unwound the braid coiled around her head. She had worn her hair that way to dinner because she had been in a mood to look cold and elegant as she stared down her retroussé nose at the earl.

Lord Lindworth, however, had not appeared to notice her or very much else at dinner. While Henry talked and Molly made polite rejoinders, the earl sat at the head of the table looking like a man with much on his mind. He barely touched his food.

He did bestir himself to inquire after her uncle, and she had informed him Uncle Brace was still unwell. She had not added it was much to her disappointment since she was anxious to leave.

"Henry said he would teach me to shoot a bow and arrow tomorrow if the weather holds. He says he is a nonpareil with a bow."

Henry would say such things. Molly did not believe modesty to be among his virtues. Still, he was agreeable, which was more than could be said for his brother or his mother. "Antonia, do not continue to scratch at your neck. You have made it quite red already."

Antonia obligingly stopped. She turned the paper over and began to draw on the other side. "If we are still here next week, Henry said—"

"We shall not be here next week!" When her cousin looked up in surprise, Molly softened her tone. "I do not mean to shout at you, but I am tired of this enforced stay."

"It is not so bad." Antonia slid off the bed and moved around the room. Since their arrival, additional pieces of furniture had been added to Molly's room. There was now a flowered wing chair by the window, a little writing desk with gilt inlay in a corner alcove, and two gleaming oak bureaus on either side of the bed.

Antonia stopped by the window and looked out. "The garden looks frightening at night. In the book I am reading, a dead cavalier haunts the garden and—" Antonia broke off and bent closer to the window. "Someone is walking among the roses in the courtyard, and he isn't even carrying a light."

97

"You are imagining it." No one would walk alone in the darkness.

"I am not! Come see."

Molly went to the window and looked down. Clouds hid the moon and made the garden even darker than usual. Spires of hedges and rounded mounds of shrubs loomed out blacker than the surrounding garden and swayed with the strong wind. "I don't see anyone."

"He has gone behind a tree. Why would anyone walk in the garden without a candle?"

Molly turned from the window. "There is no one out there. It is coming on to rain, and no one would be so foolish as to be caught out in the rain on a cool night."

"I believe it was in *Ghosts of Maramour* that someone flees through the garden in the rain."

"We are not at Maramour." Although a haunted old pile might be just as pleasant as this gracious building where the inhabitants were so disagreeable or even invisible. Lady Lindworth had yet to make an appearance.

Antonia picked up her candle. "I am going to bed. Pray watch down the hall until I reach my room."

Molly gave her cousin an indulgent smile and obliged, watching until Antonia reached her door, waved, and disappeared into her room. Molly closed her own door and sat down in the chair to read. Soon she was nodding sleepily. She knew she should get up and prepare for bed, but the bother of ringing for Frances and changing into her nightclothes kept her where she was, bound to the chair by lethargy. Her eyelids grew heavier.

Molly was awakened by a crashing sound. There it was again. Thunder. Oh, dear, Antonia would be frightened. With her young head full of hauntings and ghosts prowling gardens, she was probably under the bed right now. Molly laid aside her book and went down the hall to see to her cousin.

She knocked but received no answer.

Worried, Molly pushed open the door. She saw at a glance that the room was empty. She hurried down the hall toward the ground floor. Could Antonia have gone to the library to look at the old manuscripts again? It seemed unlikely, but Molly could not fathom where else she might have gone. Antonia was not in the library. Molly started searching the other rooms. Her concern was growing, and she had exhausted half the chambers in the sprawling lower floor before she chanced into Lord Lindworth's study.

The earl was sitting at a large table, and Antonia sat at a table nearby. She smiled up at Molly. "I was hungry and came downstairs in search of food. I stopped to say hello to the earl."

Molly glanced at Lord Lindworth, who had risen to stand politely. His eyes looked bleary and his face haggard. It was very late, but it appeared he had been working steadily. She felt a moment of sympathy for him. " 'Tis sorry I am for the intrusion, milord. I shall be taking my cousin back to her room." Molly extended a hand toward Antonia.

Antonia rose, picked up a paper, and took it to the earl. "I finished this drawing, if you need it."

He glanced disinterestedly toward the sketch, started to drop it on the table, and then froze.

Molly caught hold of Antonia's hand and they started toward the door.

"Wait!"

His command resonated around the large room.

Molly stopped. Had Antonia done something to make him angry?

He held up the drawing. "Did you do this?"

Oh, dear, Molly thought wearily, and felt Antonia's hand tighten in hers as if imploring support. "Antonia, you should not have touched his lordship's work. Apologize to him." Why was the man staring at her as if she had taken leave of her senses? Did he expect more than an apology?

If Antonia had ruined his drawing, that was too bad, but she was little more than a child, and the earl should have looked over to see what she was about instead of letting her sit there unnoticed.

"I am sorry if I did not do a good job. I thought I was helping," Antonia said meekly.

He stared at the paper. "I cannot tell which part you did and which Webber did."

Then why was he getting so agitated? Molly wondered. She thought the earl had been sitting up too late and it was affecting his reason. "Say good night to his lordship." She nudged Antonia toward the door.

"Wait. I would like a word with you, Miss Mills."

Molly put a hand on Antonia's back and gave her a gentle push out the door. "Off to bed with you." She closed the door and turned to face her host. He did not look angry, but with the English, one never knew.

"Your cousin has a great talent."

She blinked in confusion, surprised by the compliment.

He sighed. "Miss Mills, I find myself in need of someone with your cousin's skills." He gestured toward a chair. "Please, sit down so that we can talk more comfortably."

Molly sat. This conversation was not proceeding as she had imagined, and she waited with interest to see what his lordship would say next.

"Would you like a glass of wine?" he suggested.

"I should like wine, yes." As long as he was taking so long to get around to what he wanted to say, she might as well enjoy some of his expensive wine.

Chapter 6

THE EARL could be charming when he chose to be, Molly considered as she sat across from him fingering the slender stem of a hand-cut crystal glass and feeling the cool, sweet wine in her throat. She listened quietly as he explained why Antonia could be such a help to him.

"It's important that my plans be ready when the prince—" He halted and looked at her curiously. "Why are you smiling?"

" 'Tis that I see how grandly engaging you can be when you want something."

He flushed, looked down at the profusion of papers on his desk and then back up at her. "I am sorry you believe that to be true."

She smiled, softened by the wine and the gentle beating of the rain on the window. "Perhaps I am being unfair. You did take me shopping, and you have visited my uncle." When viewed in light of the fact his mother would not even quit her room, the earl was being excessively generous. "I did not mean to change the subject. You were saying you needed Antonia's help."

"Yes."

Beyond him, she saw her blurry reflection in the rain-splattered windows. "I am sure Antonia would be pleased to help." The child had little else to do. "Of course, we will not be here much longer. As soon as Uncle Brace is better, we shall leave."

"Yes, of course."

He made some more remarks, but Molly only half listened. She seldom imbibed, but the wine felt smooth and pure sliding down her throat, and the little fire in the grate was pleasant. She finished her wine and held the glass out for him to fill again. He obliged, and she settled back in the chair, playing with a loose curl on her neck and thinking that she ought to go back to bed. Instead, she asked, "Why does the prince want to build a new London?" The old one had been there hundreds of years, so one would assume it was perfectly acceptable. Dublin, the most enchanting city of Ireland, must be as old if not older than London, and it was not in need of rebuilding.

"Because he wants to leave his own stamp on the city. For all his excesses in other areas, he does have a very strong sense of beauty."

"What excesses?" she asked with gossipy interest. "Are there other things besides his mistresses and his overindulgence in food?"

The earl straightened his shoulders and said with dignity, "I was talking about the prince's interest in making London a city of greater beauty."

She finished the wine and stifled a yawn. The prince's personal life sounded more interesting. When Lord Lindworth did not immediately offer to fill her glass again, she asked, "I like the wine. Could I have some more?"

"Miss Mills, I would not wish to be the cause of you suffering tomorrow. There is also the matter," he continued delicately, "of you spending time alone with me in a remote part of the house in the middle of the night."

Shrugging, she contentedly looped a silken curl around and around her finger. Who could find fault with two people having an amicable discussion? Was the earl always this handsome? Candlelight could do amazing things to a man's face. The flames threw his countenance into shadows and peaks that hinted of mystery and even romance. Certainly the way his eyes gleamed a soft silver in the firelight was beguiling. She wound the curl tighter.

He smiled at her, and she smiled back. The chuckle that came from low in his throat was amazingly appealing. She laughed, too.

Lord Lindworth rose. "Let me escort you to your room."

"But I'm not tired."

"Perhaps not, but you will be shortly."

He stopped in front of her and offered a hand. She continued to smile at him.

He pulled her up and led her toward the door.

"I really am not tired," she told him somewhat petulantly. "I would not be objecting to another glass of wine, though."

He did not reply. He merely steered her down the hall toward the stairs.

Molly clung to him because her steps were a trifle unsteady, probably owing to the new slippers she was wearing or maybe to the fact the floor was rocking slightly. Molly had a vague recollection of the boat they had come over from Ireland in and how its rocking had affected her, and she clung more urgently to the earl.

"Are you all right, Miss Mills?" he asked.

"Well, the floor is unsteady here. You really

104

ought to see to that. Someone could fall and be hurt with a floor that moves all about like this one."

"Of course."

She looked suspiciously up at him. Was he laughing at her? No, of course not.

The stairs were difficult to navigate, but Molly thought she managed admirably. At the door of her room, he paused.

"You will have to release my arm," he said, suppressed laughter sounding in his voice.

"It was very good wine," she told him as she searched for the doorknob. Had they moved it since this afternoon? What an inconvenient thing to do. She muttered under her breath as she searched about.

He opened the door for her. "Good night."

Molly tripped into her room and closed the door behind her.

The next morning when she blinked awake and lay amidst the tumbled bedclothes, last night's events were confused in her mind. She recalled some further words, perhaps a muffled, exasperated "What a lovely nuisance." She had an even hazier memory of the earl bending and brushing a kiss on her cheek. Nothing passionate. Just a light, affectionate kiss. That, of course, must be the product of her imagination.

And the effects of the wine.

Molly rubbed at her head with the heel of her hand. She seldom drank, and she would not do so again while she was at the earl's house. She wanted to be clearheaded in all of her dealings with him.

* * *

Lord Lindworth slid down from his horse, tossed the reins to the stable boy, Charles, and started back toward the house. Puddles and a long trough of mud stood between him and the house, evidence of last night's storm. Other than that, the weather was beautiful and the sky glowed with blue charm.

The earl was in good humor as he stopped outside a side door and wiped the mud off his feet. He was relieved to have found someone to help with the drawings. There was one thing, though, that clouded his cheerfulness. He had behaved improperly last night toward Miss Mills. Yes, she had acted kittenish and coy, but he should not have stolen a kiss.

He stepped into the house and almost ran into his mother. He stepped quickly aside. "Good morning, Mother. I trust you are feeling better?"

She brushed aside the question. "Have the guests said yet when they are going to leave?" She twisted a very fine lawn handkerchief into a taut straw.

"Sir Brace is ill, Mother."

She sighed. "Yes, of course. I was so hoping he would be better by now. Who is to say when the prince might arrive?" Another sigh. "I am sure you will handle everything, Lawrence."

"Of course." How he was to accomplish that, he did not know, but right now it only mattered that he reassure his mother. "Perhaps you would like to go out today. We could make a few calls."

She brightened momentarily, then frowned. "Just you and me?"

Clearly she was afraid he would include the houseguests. "Just you and me," he told her.

She smiled. "I should like that."

Later that morning, he and his mother headed out in the carriage. Not long afterward they were shown into the little red and gold salon of Lady Danvers. The plump little dowager already had a room full of people, but she greeted Lord Lindworth and his mother with great warmth. Every face in the room turned eagerly to them, and the earl knew a sinking feeling. The gossip before they entered could well have been about them, or at least about their guests.

The teacups and hot biscuits lay forgotten on the flute-edged tea tray. The talk about clothes and children and husbands was put aside so that Mrs. Latimer could say, "Eva, you are looking perfectly wonderful." She glanced around the circle and continued, "We are all expiring to know if your guest Sir Brace is the same one who fought with the king."

Lord Lindworth kept a comforting hand around his mother's arm. "You see—" he began.

His mother laughed brightly, "Oh, no. This is someone entirely different. However could you have thought that, Mrs. Latimer?"

"Well, we had heard it was he."

"One hears all sorts of things. Are those freshly baked, Lady Danvers? You know how I adore anything your cook makes; I swear one of these days I shall hire her away from you."

"You would not, Eva. That would be too dreadful of you."

The earl took the spindly little chair offered him and sat near his mother.

Mrs. Latimer was still in pursuit of the Truth. "Now, Eva, how many Sir Braces can there be?"

"I have no idea," Lady Lindworth said innocently. She wrinkled up her nose and pondered the question. "There could be hundreds, I suppose, or thousands. It would all depend on how many mothers named their baronet sons that."

The earl had not seen his mother lie before, and he was impressed that she could do it so easily. Then he realized she had had the past few days cloistered in her room to invent stories. She had anticipated being asked this very question and had composed an answer beforehand.

The talk eventually returned to clothes and children, but not husbands, out of deference to him, he supposed.

By the time he and his mother finally rose to leave, the matter of Sir Brace had been forgotten. He handed his mother up into the carriage and climbed in after her.

"I daresay you thought it was wicked of me to be untruthful," she said guiltily.

"It did startle me," he admitted. "The fact is, in my childhood I was not always entirely truthful to you or to my nanny. I did break that vase that sat outside the study, and I did slide down the banisters and denied it when you asked me."

His mother ignored his confessions of youthful folly and continued as if to herself, "In the ordinary way of things, I would never lie. Well, occasionally about my age, but anyone who asks that question deserves to be lied to." She looked beseechingly up at him. "They will leave soon, won't they? Once they are gone, people will forget and it will not matter that I said he was another Sir Brace. If they stay, I am going to be discovered. Then there is the matter of the prince's visit. I could not endure it if they were still here then."

He reached over and patted her hand.

That seemed to relax her. "I know you will take

care of everything. You are so like your father."
She glanced around, as if to make certain there was
no one else in the carriage, before continuing,
"Henry is not yet so mature and dependable as you.
I do not wish to shock you, but I believe Henry may
go into the village some nights. I suspect he drinks
and games."

The earl suppressed a chuckle. He was certain
his brother did that and probably a deal worse. Still,
he did not wish to give his mother any further cause
for suspicion, so he only said mildly, "Henry is still
in his salad days."

"You will talk to him if there is a need for it,
won't you?"

"Of course. I would never allow him to do anything that would taint the family name. You know
that." He paused delicately before continuing, "I
know you did not invite our guests, but if you would
come to dinner just once or twice, it would make
the meals pass more pleasantly."

She blinked at him. "Dine with Sir Brace!"

"He does not leave his rooms. It is only his
daughter and his niece who come to dinner."

Lady Lindworth sniffed. "A pair of harridans, I
don't doubt."

It did not sound as if she intended to come. Lord
Lindworth let the matter drop.

Antonia popped a berry into her mouth and
reached for another. "There really are people
walled up inside rooms, you know. It happens all
the time."

"I doubt that." Molly's fingers were red with
berry stains. She had tangled with a briar a short
time ago, and it had pulled most of her hair out of

its pins. She pushed away the red locks tumbling forward as she continued plundering the berry patch. It was late in the afternoon, and she had not seen the earl today. She was glad for that even though she was sure she had imagined the kiss.

"Someone could be walled up inside the walls of this very house." Antonia looked meaningfully beyond the garden, where an old man tended the last pink roses, toward Wicklowe Hall. "It's a very old house. Frightening things often happen in such places as this. I should not be surprised if there are secret passages. It could be the earl's mother is sealed behind a wall. That might account for why we have not seen her."

"Rubbish." Molly ate another handful of berries and changed the subject. "Have you talked with your father today?"

"Yes. Poor Papa still cannot walk. I offered to read to him, but he refused. I spent some time earlier drawing for the earl. He smiled at me and said I was very good. He is not so bad for an old man."

Molly looked up, a berry poised midway to her lips. "Old?"

"Well, he must be above thirty. Even Henry is twenty-one. That's quite old, you know."

Molly smiled. "Only to someone who is thirteen. I suspect there are many young ladies in London who consider Lord Lindworth and his brother the perfect age."

"The perfect age for what?" Antonia asked as she stretched to reach a plump, juicy berry at the top of a vine.

"For marriage, of course. The earl would be an eligible partner for some woman. Just as Daniel Ryan is the perfect man for me." She reached past

Antonia, picked the berry, and handed it to her cousin.

"Do you miss Daniel?"

"Of course." Although, oddly, Molly had not thought about him much the last few days. "It will be grand to go back to Ireland and be with him again." Molly looked up at the sky. "It will be dark before long. We should return to the house to dress for dinner."

"Yes," Antonia said quickly. "I do not like to be out here after dark. Not when someone is lurking about."

"Such nonsense." Molly picked up her pail and started toward the house. In her white apron with its patchwork of pink stains and her hair tumbling down, she knew she must look like a milkmaid, but she was not likely to encounter anyone except the gardener between here and the house.

Feeling cheerful, she began to sing an Irish ballad, and Antonia picked up the tune. Pails swinging, they walked back through the roses.

Lord Lindworth was surprised to arrive in the drawing room and find Molly and Antonia already there. Antonia was pounding away on the pianoforte, and Molly was singing. He thought he had heard faint snatches of that same song coming from the garden this afternoon.

"Good evening." He was turned out to perfection in an evening coat of dark blue with gilt buttons of middling size. White unmentionables matched the gleaming whiteness of his cravat. His black hair was carefully brushed into submission, and his watch fob shone from the careful attentions of his valet.

Miss Mills wore a pink gown that matched the color in her cheeks, the little sprig of flowers in her red hair, and the tips of her fingers. Sir Brace's daughter wore a pretty white frock. Her fingers were also stained pink, he noted.

They both greeted him politely. He sat down. "You did a very fine job on the drawing," he told Antonia.

She smiled at him.

He noted that Miss Mills smiled as broadly as if he had complimented her. If she had any embarrassment about last night, it did not show. Did she not realize how inappropriate his actions had been? Surely she was not in the habit of letting men kiss her. The notion that she might be annoyed him not a little bit.

Several minutes later, Henry arrived. He was bedecked in a canary yellow coat, wine red pantaloons, and a cravat tied in such high and stiff folds that he could never lower his head. On his arm was his mother. The sight of Lady Lindworth overpowered even the canary yellow coat. She looked petite and elegant in a deep green gown. She inclined her head to her guests and waited to be introduced.

The earl did so with a smoothness that covered his surprise. He was glad she was joining them. It had grown awkward for her to keep to her rooms. He was certain she had also gotten very bored.

"I am pleased to meet you," Lady Lindworth said formally. Lawrence saw her looking at the guests' fingertips.

Molly noticed it, too. "We picked a few berries," she said with a friendly, unembarrassed smile. "I hope you do not mind."

112

"Of course not. You are welcome to whatever you please while you are here."

If that was an oblique reference to the fact they might not be here long, Molly did not seem to hear it. Instead, she nodded and murmured thanks.

Although she was trying to be polite, Lord Lindworth could feel his mother's stiffness. He was glad when dinner was announced. He escorted his mother in; Henry took Molly and returned to bring Antonia in. It was a formal method for such a small group, but the family had always done things correctly. Lawrence prided himself that they maintained such traditions when some other noble families were becoming looser in their adherence to ceremony.

Henry had once complained they should be more "modern." Lawrence had reminded his brother of the importance of being true to one's birth and station. If Lawrence did not continue to emphasize such important things, Henry was apt to behave in a manner unbefitting his family name.

The earl's gaze traveled to Miss Mills, who sat midway down the table. She looked up and saw him looking at her. Her pink gown dipped low toward her bosom, and a pearl necklace gleamed softly at her throat. She was devilishly pretty, he had to own.

Lady Lindworth, regal at the other end of the table, made distant, polite conversation with her guests about the weather and the sights in the area. "What sorts of things do you enjoy?" she asked. "If you like to watercolor, I can tell you some pretty places to go."

"We like old books," Antonia announced. "And

113

decaying old cathedrals, especially if they have ancient manuscripts in the cellars."

The dowager paused, then said tactfully, "How, er, unusual."

"My father is an authority on such matters, and he has taught Molly and me all about ancient books. He taught us how to do calligraphy, too, just as the monks did. We can even make our own ink and draw on vellum."

"What an interesting occupation for young ladies," the dowager said faintly.

Lord Lindworth lifted his glass, and the servant standing behind his chair snapped forward to refill it. Lawrence had been listening to the conversation with interest. He had not known about this peculiar occupation. It was, he supposed, more interesting than writing silly poems, as some young ladies were wont to do, or creating runny watercolors to be framed and placed in prominent positions in their papas' drawing rooms.

"Perhaps you would like to go to Stowe sometime," he said. "There is a thirteenth-century church there that is all that is left of a village that has been turned into a parkland."

Antonia smiled and nodded. Molly glanced up with interest.

His mother looked horrified. "Not that dreary old ruin, my dear."

Antonia's face lit with further excitement. "Is it haunted?"

"No."

She seemed to lose some of her enthusiasm, but Lord Lindworth saw Molly continued to look intrigued. Tomorrow he would escort her there if she wished to go. It would only take a small amount of time away from his work, and it would give him the opportunity to offer her the formal apology for the liberties he had taken yesterday. Although she did not seem to harbor any grievance against him, the rules of gentlemanly behavior dictated that he apologize.

After dessert, the men stayed for port while the ladies retired. When they joined the ladies later, Lawrence was surprised to see his mother was still present. In fact, she was sitting at a green baize faro table with thirteen cards enameled on the top. Across from her sat young Antonia. Both looked quite determined.

The one matter on which his mother was passionate was faro. She played it as if the safety of the realm depended upon whether she won. Since she was an excellent player, there was never any doubt that she would win. He only hoped Antonia was a gracious loser.

Henry paced about a bit, then excused himself to go to bed. Lawrence knew his brother would sneak out of the house in a short while and ride into town in pursuit of a more interesting game. That left Lawrence alone by the fireplace with Miss Mills. No one was near them. Now, he supposed, was as good a time as any to make an apology."

He leaned toward her and said in a low voice, "I offer my apologizes for last night."

Molly looked at him with a disconcertingly direct gaze. Didn't they teach young ladies in Ireland about keeping their lashes demurely lowered?

"So you did kiss me?" she asked.

Both of the card players looked up.

He smiled blandly over at his mother, who blinked slowly, then returned to her game. "Please keep your voice down, Miss Mills," he said, still smiling for the benefit of the others. In the same low tones he continued, "I know it was incorrect of me. I assure you it will never happen again."

"If it does, I should be sober so that I may decide if I want to kiss you."

The statement shocked him into silence. At length he intoned, "Miss Mills, the situation will not arise again."

She was still looking at him with those green eyes like deep pools lit from the bottom. "Why did you kiss me?"

He stiffened. He had assumed she would accept his apology and be too maidenly to probe further. "I beg your pardon?"

"You must have wanted to kiss me. I had drunk too much wine, but you had not."

"Miss Mills, I think this conversation has gone far enough. I acted without thought, and I beg you will forgive that. Now the matter needs to rest."

She shrugged. "I have been kissed before, you know."

He suspected her experience had not gone beyond kissing, but even that made him disgruntled. Ladies had no right to go about letting themselves be kissed. He made an abrupt change of subject. "If you and your cousin wish to see Stowe tomorrow, I shall be happy to take you there."

"Yes, I would like that. I'm sure Antonia would, too."

From across the room came Antonia's gleeful shout. "I won!"

The earl looked over to see his mother rising from the table with a stunned look. Antonia beamed.

"I never lose," Lady Lindworth said dully, as if

by stating this, she could change the outcome of the game.

"You lost this time," Antonia pointed out tactlessly.

Lady Lindworth looked down at the cards as if they had betrayed her. Then she took a wounded leave.

In the distance the earl heard hoofbeats and realized Henry was flying toward town. He suppressed a sigh. This had not been a good evening. First Miss Mills's disconcerting frankness about his kiss, and now his mother's pride was wounded. She might well disappear into her rooms for several more days. Lawrence rose to start to his study. He could at least get in a few hours of work before retiring for the evening. Tomorrow he hoped things went more smoothly.

Chapter 7

THE OVERCONSUMPTION of berries had a bad effect on Antonia, who awoke the next morning with an aching stomach. After giving her tonic and suggesting plenty of rest, Molly left her cousin in the capable hands of Frances and went downstairs to join the earl.

He was standing in the hall wearing a wine-colored coat with a single row of silver buttons, and gray pantaloons. The little tassels on his Hessians swung sharply as he straightened at her entry.

"Antonia is ill and will not be joining us." Molly stopped in front of him and brushed back the wayward curls dancing around her cheekbones.

"We cannot go alone in a closed carriage."

"We went into town without a chaperon," she reminded him.

"That was in an open vehicle and only for a short distance."

"My maid is staying with Antonia. Unless your mother wishes to accompany us, there is no one else." Molly smiled innocently, knowing his mother would not deign to accompany them.

Judging from the stiff expression on the earl's face, he did not intend to invite her. After a moment he said, "I shall be back momentarily."

It was closer to ten minutes before Lord Lindworth returned with a bemused-looking Henry trailing beside him.

"I had other plans," Henry mumbled.

"Yes, yes," his brother said dismissingly. "We should not be gone long."

"Not long?" Henry looked confused. "Thought I saw the servants putting a picnic lunch into the carriage."

"Do not concern yourself with that." Lawrence bundled his brother out the door. Molly followed.

Molly thought any illusions Lord Lindworth had about his brother's abilities as a chaperon must have been dashed five minutes later when Henry fell soundly asleep and began to snore. Still, he was there, sitting on the seat next to the earl and slumping against the side of the carriage. So everything was according to the English sense of propriety, she supposed.

The earl glanced at his brother, then sighed. "I daresay Henry was up late last night."

"No doubt." She had heard Henry returning at three in the morning.

In a pointed move to change the subject, Lord Lindworth said, "Tell me about your interest in old manuscripts."

Molly studied him. "Do you ask out of politeness or from a desire to know? My answer will depend on yours." She could not prevent a smile. "If you are genuinely interested, I shall tell you about the Book of Kells and how it was found hidden in a bog, no doubt placed there by monks trying to protect it from invaders. I shall talk to you about Carolingian minuscules, or small letters, that became accepted during the reign of Charlemagne in the ninth century. I will tell you the life story of a man from Mainz named Johann Gutenberg, who devised a movable type on a wooden press and made it possible to print thousands of books. If, however, you are only asking because you can think of no other conversation, I shall simply say I like to run my fingers over pages written hundreds of years ago by some poor, forgotten man struggling to keep learning alive." Take that, milord.

"I see."

They hit a bump, which caused Henry to blink awake. "Are we there yet?" he mumbled.

"No, go back to sleep."

Henry obliged and was soon snoring again.

Molly looked from one brother to the other. Had the earl ever been as careless and carefree as Henry? She doubted it. Lord Lindworth seemed to have been schooled in the responsibility of his position until he was a prisoner to duty. Poor man. Did he know what fun there was to be had by those willing to forget their pride now and again?

Molly opened her window and put her face out to the wind. The gentle breeze felt good blowing across her cheeks. The day was full of high white clouds and fresh breezes blowing through the green trees that lined the narrow road.

"There is an old church not far from here," the earl said. "The roof was crumpling, so it has to be restored. I heard they had uncovered some old books in the cellar. We could stop to see them if you like."

While Ireland had many ancient churches, she had not yet been in any English churches. "Yes, please."

Henry was fast asleep when they turned down the lane leading to the church. Vines curled across the road in places, and Molly held her breath as they crossed a fragile, swaying bridge. The church itself was surrounded by beeches that flanked its tiny steeple. Little round windows of stained glass peeked out of the small church, giving it the look of a miniature cathedral. Molly was enchanted. Henry continued to snore as the earl handed her out of the carriage. They left him there.

Lord Lindworth helped Molly down a path of weedy flagstones to the main entrance. No carts or horses were in sight; the workman must be taking the day off.

Molly ventured into the vestibule. "It's cool in here."

"If you would like to leave, we can."

"I am not complaining." The shafts of sunlight that made their way through the surrounding trees glinted through the red and blue and gold glass and sent prisms of color bouncing around the little chapel. The old pews sat empty and expectant, as if waiting for people to crowd in.

"It's very pretty," she whispered.

"Yes," the earl agreed in a quiet voice.

Molly always felt reverent and awed in churches. Lord Lindworth seemed to feel the same.

He kept his hand on her arm as they walked up the center aisle to a door that led downward into darkness. The earl had had the foresight to bring a candle. He lit it now and held it above his head as he led the way down a winding staircase into an old cellar. Molly held her skirts with one hand and clung to a rickety metal banister with the other.

Down in the cellar, she peered around and saw a sarcophagus fitted into a niche in the wall. An old altar sat in another corner, and atop it stood a massive book. Molly started forward and carefully touched the book. It was bound with a plain oaken board cover. The pages were thick vellum, and each new page began with an elaborately constructed capital letter. The letter A was fitted around an angel.

She glanced at the earl and murmured, "It is a splendid book." It was not as old or as ornate as many, but she knew that Ireland held the bulk of the truly great manuscripts. This ancient text was certainly an unexpected find in a remote English church. It made her wonder if a monastery had stood nearby or if a terrified priest hundreds of years ago had hid the book here and stood quivering while he waited for an onslaught of some marauding tribe to pass.

Lord Lindworth held the candle aside so as not to drip wax on the book. That left Molly and the earl standing close together with only a faint light to share. His hand was still on her arm, warm against the dry chill of the cellar. She smelled candle wax and the starch from his cravat. Then a draft put the candle out and left them in sudden, utter darkness.

He tightened his hold on her arm. "Don't be afraid."

Of course, she was not afraid. Did he think she was some fainting maiden who went fluttery at the least thing? "I am perfectly fine," she informed him briskly.

"Drat, where is my tinderbox?"

Something clattered to the floor. "I think you just dropped it."

He muttered to himself, and Molly smiled. She

would warrant the staid earl had not been in this situation before.

After a moment he said, "We shall have to find our way without a light. Can you manage?"

"Certainly."

"I shall go first. Hold on to me." She took his hand. Although she was not afraid, his hand felt warm and reassuring as he began to walk. She followed, stepping carefully on the packed earth floor. Molly had not taken two steps before stumbling on the uneven floor and landing squarely against his lordship's back. She giggled.

"Why are you laughing?" he demanded curtly.

"I was thinking it is a pity Antonia is not here bumbling around in the darkness. She would see ghosts rising out of the crypts and hear people who are walled up behind the walls calling to us."

"Your cousin has a rich imagination. Here, give me your hand. It will be safer."

Molly put her hand in his large one. Suddenly, wickedness overcame her and she said, "Where is your hand, Lord Lindworth? I cannot find it in the dark."

There was a startled pause. "Then whose hand am I holding?"

"I don't know," she whispered in horror.

She felt him stiffen, then he snapped, "Miss Mills, I do not find your attempt at humor amusing."

Sighing, she said, "Yes, it is my hand you are holding, but don't you find it exciting to be frightened now and again?"

"No, I do not."

"Do you mean on stormy nights when the wind howls down, you never hid beneath the covers and imagined witches riding on the wind? Not even as a boy?"

"Of course not," he said with asperity.

"How dull."

"My entertainment lies in more intelligent pursuits like architecture."

"Humph."

He drew her toward the stairs. Molly admitted he had a sure step in the darkness. Still, not to ever want to be deliciously scared was unthinkable.

Finally they reached the top step and were again in the chapel. The light spilling through the stained-glass windows looked brilliant after the darkness. "It is a beautiful church, and I'm glad I got to see the old manuscript, if only briefly." The earl had a cobweb on the back of his perfect wine red coat, but Molly did not pluck it off. She thought it made him look rather more human. She was certain, though, that his valet would faint when he discovered it.

They went out into the sunlight and back to the carriage, where Henry still slept. He roused himself as they climbed in.

Blinking vagely, he mumbled, " 'Lo. Did I miss anything?"

"A ghost," Lord Lindworth said dryly.

Henry's eyes opened wide. "Really?"

Ignoring him, the earl gave directions to the driver to proceed. Henry was fully awake now. "I am hungry. What did Cook pack?"

Molly looked up with interest. She would not object to a morsel of food herself. The earl must have noticed her expression, for he said, "There is a pretty view not far from here. We can stop there and eat."

Molly settled back to wait while Henry straight-ened in the seat and adjusted his jacket with as much attention as if he thought crowds of fashion-able people would be gathered when they stopped in the middle of nowhere.

"This is it," Lord Lindworth announced after they had driven a short distance.

Molly looked out her window and caught her breath. "It is charming," she told the earl as he handed her down.

The little overlook had a grassy spot level enough to spread out a cover to sit on and arrange the food on a separate cover. The ground sloped down gently a few feet across a carpet of clover, and then chalk cliffs fell off sharply, affording a view of juniper and spindle dotting the flinty floors of the valley far be-low. A horse in the field looked like a child's toy.

The driver and footman took the basket out of the carriage and spread out the food while Molly walked a few feet down the grassy slope to stand near the precipice. She turned her face upward and let the sun kiss it while a breeze caught at her skirts.

"Are we ready to eat now?" Henry asked plain-tively. "I am near to famished."

Molly walked back up the hill and sat down to cheese and fruits and bread that was still warm from the morning's baking. She placed a linen nap-kin over her skirts.

The three talked about inconsequential matters while they ate. The weather was fine, all agreed. London was a superb city that Molly would enjoy enormously, Henry assured her. Antonia would not suffer sickness from the berries long, Lord Lind-worth ventured. Nothing of significance was said, but Molly felt content sitting alongside the two brothers. When he was relaxed, the earl was a good companion. He was not like some men who talked only of themselves. He asked her questions about herself and about Ireland.

After they had eaten and the servants were packing up, Lawrence excused himself to walk down the road to look at the crumbling remains of an abandoned manor house to inspect its architecture.

Molly watched her host striding down the road with long, sure steps. She found she had a greater interest in him than before and turned to Henry to ask, "How did your brother become interested in architecture?" A man in his position did not have to work, yet he had chosen to do so instead of spending his days at drinking clubs and his nights with mistresses. She respected the earl for doing something useful with his time.

Henry shrugged. "A fire a few years back burned some cottages on the estate. Instead of simply rebuilding, he wanted to make better, more comfortable houses for the tenants."

"That was thoughtful." And surprising. Not that she believed the earl uncaring about others, but such consideration was unlooked-for.

"He isn't a bad sort. He even designed an orphanage and paid for it with his own blunt." Henry followed up this praise by adding, "He is still out of temper with me about the gypsy and the furniture. I am going to make everything right, though." Henry smiled mysteriously.

"Oh? How are you going to accomplish that?"

"I have ways. You didn't think I went out every night to drink and gamble, did you?"

Molly had thought precisely that and said so.

He looked at her with wounded pride. "Nothing of the sort. I have been busy making inquiries. I have friends helping me."

"What does your brother think of your efforts?"

"He does not know. I want to surprise him. You must not tell him."

Molly nodded. She suspected Henry was bragging to impress her. His inquiries probably consisted of wandering around the local alehouse announcing what actions he would take if he ever caught the gypsy. Lord Lindworth had hired Mr. Miller to find the gypsy, and if he was ever found, she was sure it would be through Mr. Miller.

"Lawrence is so worried about the prince's visit, I don't want to distract him. It's a good thing your cousin is able to help him. Lawrence could use half a dozen more who can draw as well as she."

Molly plucked a blade of grass and pulled it lazily through her fingers. Her own skills were far superior to Antonia's. Should she offer Lord Lindworth her assistance?

"Antonia may grow restless," Henry added. "She devils me to take her out practicing with a bow, so I am not sure how much longer Lawrence can keep her interested in his tedious drawings."

Henry might be right. It would be the kind and gracious thing for her to help the earl. She would tell him of her decision to help on the way back to the estate.

Lord Lindworth returned a short time later. As the carriage swayed back toward the house and Henry dozed beside his brother, Molly smiled at her host and said, "I have decided to assist you with the drawings you are making for the king."

Instead of the enthusiasm she had anticipated,

he hesitated, then said, "They must be very well drawn."

"Yes, I know. I am quite good."

He blinked, taken aback by her words.

"Do Englishwomen not present themselves so forthrightly?" She put both hands on the seat beside her to steady herself as they rounded a sharp corner, but she kept her eyes on him.

"They are reticent to appear overly proud."

"Honesty is superior to false modestly." She tossed her head, causing her bonnet to slip back until it dangled behind her by its strings. As she righted her bonnet, she demanded, "Do you need help or not, milord?"

He held himself stiffly erect, no small accomplishment in the swaying carriage. "Yes."

"Then I am going to help you."

"Very well." They both turned to look out opposite windows, and neither spoke the remainder of the journey.

Lord Lindworth was not in the habit of doing nothing, yet he found himself sitting in the parlor after dinner, and long after everyone had left, gazing disinterestedly into the popping fire and mulling over the afternoon's events. Miss Mills had behaved in a shockingly forward manner. No other lady of his acquaintance would have been so insistent in her offer. Irish ladies, particularly Miss Mills, would never fit into society here.

He thought of young Antonia, and for a moment he felt sorry for her. Her father wanted her admitted into the drawing rooms and parlors of the ton, but that would never happen. Aside from Sir Brace's own transgression, there was the matter of

Antonia's training. She would not know how to go on. He doubted she could be shy and demure any more than her cousin could.

Lawrence lifted his head at the sound of hoof-beats. That would be Henry off on his nightly journey. Rising, Lawrence paced around the room. He was bored even though he had plenty to do. Yet some unnamed restlessness kept him from proceeding to his study and resuming his work. He had jumbled thoughts about the day's events. Mostly, though, he looked back with wonder at how much he had enjoyed himself. He had made the trip out of a sense of duty and had been surprised to find he enjoyed Miss Mills's company so much. In fact, he often endured strained conversation with young ladies who spoke only about their ball gowns or the last soiree they had attended. Miss Mills's conversation had been more interesting. There was certainly nothing unpleasant about gazing into a pair of clear green eyes that were the centerpoint of a very pretty face.

Drat, why couldn't he concentrate on his work? He circled the room a time or two and then started out the door. He would go into town to the ale-house. A smile swept over his face as he realized the shock it would give Henry to see him in that low retreat. Well, a glass or two of bad stout and the company of raucous tradesmen might be what he needed to distract him.

He went up to his room and announced his intentions to his valet. That man, after paling visibly, nodded bravely and assisted his master into a double-breasted riding coat and long trousers. Lawrence waited impatiently for the valet to button the buttons on his ankles.

"It is not my business, of course, milord, but is anything amiss?" the valet asked as he rose and began brushing the coat.

"Nothing."

The valet looked grieved as Lord Lindworth started out the door.

Even Lawrence's horse, Hecate, appeared startled to be led out of her stall at this hour of the night. However, she offered a spirited ride into town, slowing only when they reached the inn yard, where noise and laughter spilled out through the open door. The earl dismounted and went inside.

He glanced past the knots of farmers and yeomen to where Henry sat at a table, flanked by a pair of large men. The three were merrily quaffing ale from thick glasses when he approached.

Henry saw him, and his glass came down hard on the table. " 'S blood, Lawrence, what are you doing here?" The earl glanced at the giants on either side of his brother and recognized Edgar Willoughby, the squire's son. The other man was a stranger.

"Joining you for a drink, Henry," Lawrence announced, and sat down.

Henry blinked. "She didn't tell you anything, did she?"

"Who tell me what?"

Henry looked away."It doesn't signify."

Lord Lindworth let the remark pass. He had come here for distraction, not to argue with his brother. Still, his curiosity was piqued. He thought "she" might be Miss Mills. What had Henry asked her not to tell?

Henry was already signaling the proprietor over. "Drinks for m' brother, and be quick about it."

A few people recognized the earl and looked at him with curiosity. He had not been seen in here since his own youthful days, but the place had changed little, unfortunately.

"I understand you had the devil's own time getting your property back, Lord Lindworth," Edgar said.

The earl drank from the glass set in front of him and nodded in response to the question.

"I expect you would like to see the scoundrel brought to task for his crime." Edgar winced. "Who kicked me?"

Henry changed the subject. "I understand Miss Mills is going to help you with your drawings. That's very kind of her."

Lord Lindworth took another drink without replying. Something was afoot here, and he wished he knew what it was.

"Is Miss Mills the redheaded woman?" the stranger asked. "Saw her in town the other day. Built well. I've heard she is spirited as well. I like a woman with spirit."

Lord Lindworth stared at the square-faced, ham-fisted man. He made Molly Mills sound like a horse. "The lady is my guest," he said stiffly. "I will thank you to bear that in mind and refrain from discussing her in such terms." As an afterthought he said, "I do not believe we have met before."

"Giles Glancy," Henry said quickly. "From Dover."

"Dover? You are a long way from home." What the hell was he doing here in the middle of the night drinking ale with Henry and the dim-witted Edgar?

"He is only stopping on his way through," Henry said.

Couldn't the man speak for himself? The earl surveyed his brother and decided the three men were plotting some foolish mission like riding with the mail coach. Tomorrow he would talk to Henry. He did not want his brother doing anything to embarrass the family—not when the prince was expected any day. Henry had had his youthful folly with the gypsy; now it was time to be responsible.

Mysterious friends from Dover and secrets with Miss Mills were going to stop. The Prince of Wales was coming to visit, and they must act as befitted people of their station. Lawrence meant to make certain Henry understood that.

Chapter 8

THE NEXT morning Molly rose early, allowed Frances to help her into a simple white gown and brush her hair until it shone in the light, then proceeded with her maid downstairs to the earl's study. Lord Lindworth rose courteously as Molly breezed into the room. She carried with her a little carved box of drawing supplies.

"Antonia is sleeping late, but I have come to help with the sketches. My maid," she pointed out, "is accompanying me."

She thought she heard a sigh, but ignored it. Instead, she began laying out her supplies on the secretary's desk while her maid sat by the window and took out her mending. When Molly had everything arranged on the desk, she smiled at the earl. "What do you wish me to do first?"

He brought over a blank sheet of paper. "You can start by drawing a border."

"What sort of border will you be wanting?"

"Anything you like."

Molly took the paper wordlessly. It was plain he was giving her a simple task to test her. She did not voice any objections. If the earl doubted her word, she would prove to him that she was as good as she said.

She began drawing Greek columns down each side of the paper. Then she decorated the tops of the columns with acanthus leaves. Along the bottom and top she drew simple, straight lines, adding the royal crest in the center at the bottom. When she was done, she inspected her work with satisfaction. She looked up. "I am finished."

Lord Lindworth came over and looked at the drawing. Slowly he raised his eyes to meet hers. "You really are good. Quite good."

The wonder in his voice and the admiration in his gray eyes pleased her. "Yes, I told you."

A grin tugged at the corners of his mouth. "You did indeed. I should have listened."

The maid glanced up, and Molly ignored her reproving look. Modesty was all very well and good, but so was honesty. She saw no reason to hide her abilities.

"Let me give you some buildings to sketch in." He left and returned with a large sheet of paper. Pleased to tackle something more challenging, she set to work.

Two hours later, Frances had nodded off in the corner, but Molly was diligently adding an upper row of windows to a sketch.

The earl looked over at her with a guilty expression. "You are free to leave at any time, Miss Mills. I do not want to keep you from other plans."

Molly brushed back the curls falling out of their pins and shook her head. "I have no other plans. I enjoy taking the rough drawings and turning them into quality renderings. Besides, you need help, don't you?"

"Yes."

"Well, then, I shall continue working." Molly

pulled the rest of the pins from her hair and let the curls fall. It was easier than constantly pushing pins back in. She thought she noticed the earl glance in her direction as the red curls fell free, but she kept on working.

Outside the window she heard Antonia's shouts. Her cousin must be in the meadow engaging in a game of archery with Henry. At another time, Molly might have been tempted to join them, but now she was content where she was.

Engrossed in her task, she started to hum, then caught herself. "Does my humming disturb you?"

He shook his head. "Not in the least. I rather like it."

Molly blinked. She did not have an exceptional voice, but she liked to hum, and it pleased her that the earl did not object. Even Daniel made no secret of the fact her humming annoyed him. Smiling, she lowered her lashes. With renewed dedication, she returned to her work.

Half an hour later, she lifted her head to ask which direction a building faced in relation to the other buildings.

Lord Lindworth came over and stood behind her chair, pointing with square-tipped fingers at the buildings and explaining, "Once they are laid out together, they will form a sweeping semicircle."

Molly looked up at him, gazing up past the firm notch of his chin and into those gray eyes shaded by their thick fringe of lashes. While he explained symmetry in architecture, she irreverently thought about his kiss. If he was going to kiss her, she wished it could have been when she was sober so that she could recall the details with greater accuracy.

He was in the middle of describing how windows evolved from narrow slits designed to keep out arrows when he suddenly broke off. "I am boring you."

"No," she said quickly. "Well, perhaps I am not so interested in the history of architecture, but I like to listen to you because you are so passionate about it. I understand that. No one knows why I want to recopy old manuscripts that have been moldering in crypts for hundreds of years, but it interests me the way this interests you. I suppose everyone has something that pulls at his fancy."

"Yes."

When they each returned to their tasks, the atmosphere between them felt more companionable.

It was two more hours before Molly rose. "I should go see Uncle Brace."

The earl rose politely, and the maid, hearing movement, roused herself from sleeping. "Thank you, Miss Mills. You have accomplished a great deal, and I am most appreciative."

She smiled at him. His answering smile was so pleasant and friendly that she almost sat down to continue working. But her back was stiff, and she really felt obliged to look in on her uncle.

"You are quite welcome, Lord Lindworth."

Molly did not look back as she left the room, but she knew he was watching her. She nodded in satisfaction and continued on down to her uncle's door while Frances started back to Molly's room. Molly found Uncle Brace asleep, so she went up the stairs and knocked on Antonia's door.

As Molly stepped into the room, she saw Antonia sitting on the floor by the window, her blue kersey-mere skirts spread out around her, and a paper on her lap. Antonia shoved the paper into a book and then looked up with a wide, innocent smile. Too innocent, Molly thought.

"Busy, Antonia?" she asked casually.

"Just writing a few letters."

Molly closed the door and looked toward the book. "Secret letter?" She did not wish to pry into her cousin's affairs, but she was curious why Antonia hid the paper from her. Antonia kept very little from her.

Antonia hesitated, then leaned forward to confide, "I daresay I can tell you. I am penning a letter to the gypsy, William Jersey. You remember, he is the man who removed the furnishings from the house and took them to Bath."

Molly crossed to sit on the floor beside her cousin. She was certain that English ladies did not sit on floors, even beautiful, polished parquet floors like this one, but she did. "Why would you be doing that?"

"It was Henry's idea. We are going to lure William Jersey back here and then spring a trap on him." Antonia clapped her hands together like the jaws of a trap springing shut.

"He is never going to return here."

"That's the splendid part! In the letter I pretend to be one of the maids, Letty, who was smitten with him. I write to say the furniture has been returned and one of the chests contained an ancient manuscript hidden in a secret compartment. The binding is in gold and it is encrusted with rare jewels."

Molly looked doubtful. "Why would the maid write to tell him that?"

"I told you, she had formed a *tendre* for him. The maid no longer works here, but William Jersey does not know that. We are going to enclose a page from the book. If the bait is strong enough, Henry believes the gypsy is greedy enough to sneak back."

"How can you send a page if there is no book?" Molly asked.

"I'm going to make one. Unless," she added in pleading accents, "you would write a page. You are ever so much better than I am."

The plan seemed full of pitfalls to Molly, not the least of which was knowing where to find the thief. "How do you know where to send the letter?"

"There is a gypsy encampment near St. Birinus Hill, not far from here. We will get the letter to them, and they are certain to know how to send it along. William Jersey may even be there."

"It seems a gamble."

Antonia straightened on the floor. "Henry must try. It is the only way to redeem himself to his brother and to show Lord Lindworth that Henry really is brilliant."

Molly forbore to comment on Henry's brilliance. Instead, she murmured, "I am surprised Henry cares so much what his brother thinks of him."

"Henry says Lawrence is not so bad. Lawrence is good to his tenants, and he gives Henry funds out of his own money because Henry does not have a large trust."

"That is kind," she agreed.

"Yes. Henry said his brother still supports a woman he once had in keeping because she has no other income and she is sick and cannot work."

Molly looked at her cousin. "Henry certainly makes bold in his conversation with you."

Antonia giggled. "He did not say that to *me*. I

verheard him talking with someone else. Still, I think it a kind thing for Lord Lindworth to do."

Molly did not reply. She should not be shocked to learn the earl had had women in keeping. Many men of his station kept what they referred to as a high-flyer. Certainly Lord Lindworth was charitable to give money to someone in need. Did he have someone in keeping now? she wondered. She was disappointed to think that he might.

"Of course, Henry does not believe Lawrence will continue to support her once he is married."

Molly looked up in true surprise. "Lord Lindworth is getting married?"

"No. At least, he has not proposed to any woman, but Henry says it is time he did. Since the earl is so aware of his duty and his need to produce an heir, Henry believes he will choose a bride this Season or the next."

Molly felt unaccountably relieved. "It sounds as if Henry gives more thought to his brother's affairs than he does to his own," she observed dryly. Still, she had to own to a certain curiosity toward the earl herself.

"Oh, no. Henry has his own future to think about. He is very serious about riding with the Four-in-Hand Club, and he intends to make the Grand Tour of the continent next year. Still, the earl's marriage is important to the whole family. Lord Lindworth is maddeningly particular, but I daresay a man in his position cannot settle for just any little nobody."

"You are beginning to sound like the English, Antonia." Or someone who had spent too much time with Lady Lindworth playing cards.

"I am English," her cousin reminded her loftily.

Yes, Molly reflected. That was why they had come here in the first place. Uncle Brace wanted his only daughter to have a chance in society. Molly did not think that was any more possible now than it had been when they stepped off the boat from Ireland. She wondered if Uncle Brace realized as much.

"Why are you frowning? Is something wrong?" Antonia asked.

"No." An idea was forming in her mind as Molly rose from the floor and brushed her hands over her skirts. "Be sure to look in on your father before dinner."

"I will. Molly, you will write a page to enclose in the letter, won't you?"

"Yes." It seemed a harmless enough act.

Molly smiled at her and pulled the door closed. As she headed down the hall, she thought about Antonia being kept outside the closed doors of society. Would it help to open those doors if she talked with Lord Lindworth about Antonia? He might not be able to assure admittance to the likes of Almack's, but he might be able to suggest some dance masters and chaperons who had an entree into society. After dinner this evening, she would try to draw the earl aside and speak with him.

With that in mind, she waited impatiently through a meal of endless courses. As soon as dinner ended, Lady Lindworth and Antonia returned to the card table, with Antonia looking confident and Lady Lindworth looking vengeful.

That left Molly to amuse herself until the gentlemen finished their port and joined the ladies again. The men had not been back in the room above fifteen minutes before Henry mumbled some excuses and left. Molly was relieved to see him go.

"I am glad we are alone," she confided to Lord Lindworth as they sat on the red settees flanking the fireplace. His mother and Antonia occupied the other end of the long room.

The earl's expression turned watchful. "Why?"

"I have a favor to ask." Molly plunged on. "You know Uncle Brace wants Antonia to have the advantages of any other well-bred English girl." She paused for his reply.

"Yes," he said cautiously.

"I was thinking that there must be women who have lost their fortunes or even someone who is kindhearted who would agree to take Antonia to a few parties and routs."

He shook his head. "Miss Mills, a Season is much more complex than that."

"Antonia does not have to be the belle of the Season. Uncle Brace only wants her to catch the eye of an eligible man. A younger son would be perfectly acceptable and—" She broke off. "Why are you looking at me as if my wits have gone begging?"

"Because you appear to believe the London Season is a marriage mart open to all interested young ladies. It is not. The Ton is an exclusive club, and one must have entrée. Not to put too fine a point on it, but a gentleman requires a wife of good countenance, a suitable dowry, and impeccable breeding."

"That's all very well for a duke, but what about the youngest son in a family of twelve? He must marry someone. Surely he does not have the same requirements."

The stern lines around his mouth flexed, and a smile broke through. "Miss Mills, I have never seen anyone as stubborn as you. If you were a man, you would probably have been shot in a duel by now."

"I am not a man," she informed him.

"No, you are not," he said in slow, thoughtful tones.

The atmosphere between them seemed to change subtly. They were no longer talking about Antonia and her future, Molly realized. Somehow they were now talking about Molly, and the earl was looking at her with speculative eyes.

"Please try to think if you know anyone who could help get Antonia presented," Molly said briskly.

He started to shake his head, then paused and examined the signet ring gleaming on his finger in the light from the fire. "I give no promises, but I shall make inquiries."

"Splendid."

She wondered briefly why he was willing to do this. The thought occurred to her that he was doing it as a favor to her, and that touched her.

Lawrence tracked Henry to earth in his room and asked bluntly, "Who was the man from Dover?"

"Giles Glancy."

"Yes, you told me his name earlier. I am curious why he was here and what you and he may be scheming together."

Henry managed a look of affront, but the earl did not find it very convincing. Lawrence sighed. "Henry, the king's son will arrive any day. Mother is already distraught about our company. Pray do not add to her worries by doing anything foolish beyond repair."

"I have no intention of doing anything foolish," Henry huffed.

Lawrence smiled. "Good."

Henry unbent enough to smile back. "So Mother is still overset by the guests? I thought she might come to like them. I do not know Sir Brace very well, but his daughter and niece are pleasant enough."

"Mother is determined not to like them."

"Ah, well." Henry turned to leave, then casually turned back. "I may be gone a day or so, Lawrence."

"Oh, where do you mean to go?" the earl asked with an indifference to match his brother's.

"Just over to Charlbury to see a bit of blood a man has for sale."

A horse? Since when did Henry have the thousand guineas it took to buy the sort of horseflesh he would choose?

The question lingered on Lawrence's mind as he walked about on the small terrace beside the dining room and smoked a cheroot. Then he started for his study to put the finishing touches on an arch over a thoroughfare on one of the last drawings.

He opened the door and stopped in midstride. Miss Mills was standing over the secretary's desk. She started when she saw him. "I—I left some pencils I needed to complete work on something else."

Was it his imagination or did she look guilty? "It is almost midnight. Surely you are not working at this hour?"

"I—well, I could not sleep, and I thought a bit of drawing might relax me." She laughed rather feebly. "You came here to work, so it cannot be all that late."

"That is true." He didn't want to talk about him
self, though. He was far more curious and skeptical
about her. Lawrence remained standing in the
doorway. Having just come from a conversation
with Henry, the earl had the uncomfortable suspi
cion no one in the house was telling him the truth
about anything. He lounged against the doorframe
blocking her path. "I should like to see some of your
other work, Miss Mills."

She busied herself searching for her writing in-
struments again. "It is nothing. Just a means to
while away the hours."

"I see."

She looked up at him then. The light glinted off
the windows and reflected around the room, making her look soft and pretty. Her hair hung loose
and carefree, and her eyes held the glow from the
candlelight. As he gazed at her, he wondered why
he had ever preferred blue-eyed women.

A clap of thunder sounded, and Molly looked toward the window. "Antonia will be frightened. I
should go to her before she takes refuge under the
covers."

He did not move from his position by the door.
He was unsatisfied by her explanation of why she
was here, but that was not the whole reason he remained fixed where he was. He was also reluctant
to see her go.

"You yourself pointed out the merits of burrow-
ing beneath the covers."

She watched him apprehensively. Was he so
threatening or did she have something to hide?

"There are times when it is thrilling to be a little
frightened." She moved toward the door. "I do not
mean to keep you from your work."

"The halls are dark, Miss Mills. I will escort you back to your room. Unless," he suggested with a mocking smile, "you are in a mood to be deliciously frightened?"

"Thunder does not frighten me, Lord Lindworth."

He inclined his head to one side. "What does?"

"Runaway horses."

"There should not be any in the halls, but I will accompany you just to make certain."

Molly gave him her arm. He noticed she seemed small and fragile gliding along beside him in the murky halls while each of them held a candle aloft for light.

"Why runaway horses?" he asked curiously at the bottom of the staircase.

"When I was a little girl, I was in the carriage with my mother when someone fired a gun and the horses bolted. Mother was thrown out, leaving me in the carriage alone. I was terrified. It seemed to me that the horses ran for miles. They trampled a hedge. I remember seeing the hedge coming up toward me and then being buried in it and feeling the branches scratch at my face and arms. . . ." She stopped and glanced at him. "Forgive me. I didn't mean to talk at such length."

He did not object. In fact, he had listened attentively to the rise and fall of her words. He had heard the fear that still echoed through after all these years.

"Were you injured?" he asked.

"Just the scratches. The horses finally plunged into a river, and a ferryman dragged me out."

At the door of her room, she turned to him. "I shall be down to continue work in the morning."

"Thank you, Miss Mills."

After her door closed, he went slowly down the steps back to his study. His houseguest was a curious creature. Pretty and proud and headstrong, she could also be vulnerable and caring. Certainly she cared for her cousin and her uncle. Lawrence had not wanted Miss Mills to come, but in a strange way, the house was richer for her presence. Her lilting words floated down the halls, and her smile lit any room she graced.

He drew himself up stiffly. He sounded like a man besotted instead of a man who had work to complete and no time to think about Irishwomen.

Molly labored late into the night creating the page for Henry. She took great care to make it look like one a monk might have drawn hundreds of years ago. As she worked, she heard the rain slap against her windowpane.

She knew the earl was suspicious about her late night need for the pens. She did not think she had convinced him. She hoped he did not press her further, because she did not like lying to him.

It was still raining the next morning when she gave the page to Henry. She heard him ride away a short time later.

Then, dressed simply in a scoop-necked pearl white gown, she went down to the earl's large study and applied herself to the tasks there. Antonia, who was also a prisoner of the rain, labored beside her.

That afternoon the rain stopped, and the two of them went for a walk through the garden. Afterward Molly and Antonia repaired to the drawing room. They had not been there above five minutes when Lady Lindworth appeared. Although she held playing cards at the ready, she feigned indifference as to whether Antonia wished to play.

Antonia, who could not go outside to practice her archery, was more than happy to oblige. They moved to the green baize game table and began to play.

"Do ghosts leave footprints?" Antonia asked.

"There are no such things as ghosts," Lady Lindworth replied starchily. "Do you intend to play that card or not?"

"I am still thinking."

Molly glanced up from her book and could not repress a smile.

Antonia started to place a card, then drew it back up. "Well, I saw a ghost walking in the courtyard last night in the rain, and this morning there were footprints."

"Impossible. The only way to reach the courtyard is from the house. No one would be addlepated enough to go out and walk in the rain."

Molly looked thoughtfully toward the door. She had just come from visiting Uncle Brace, who had declared himself miserable with gout. Yet she had seen a pair of shoes in the corner by the door with what looked suspiciously like mud on them. Was it possible her uncle was not being honest with her? Of course, Molly reflected, the earl's study also led out onto the courtyard. He had worked late last night and might have gone out for a walk.

It was more likely that Antonia was wrong about seeing someone outside. After all, her mind was full of tales from the books she read. If Uncle Brace did go out, though, it seemed possible the earl had seen him. Molly wondered if her uncle was fooling all of them with his tales of gout.

Was there a tactful way to discover from Lord Lindworth if he had seen anyone in the courtyard without casting doubt on her uncle?

Rising and brushing off her skirts, Molly decided to try to find out. She left her book on the needle-pointed chair and excused herself to Antonia and Lady Lindworth. Neither gave the slightest sign she had spoken.

"I have the ace!" Antonia was chortling.

"A lady does not gloat," Lady Lindworth informed her.

"You did when you won the other day."

Their voices receded in the distance as Molly followed the long corridors until she turned down the hall to the earl's study. She found him seated over a single candle, hard at work, with drawings spread out on the floor around him. He looked up when she entered.

She smiled cheerfully. "Before you give me a scold about being here without a chaperon, let me assure you I only mean to stay a minute."

He rose and waited politely.

It belatedly occurred to Molly she did not even have a trumped-up excuse to use to talk to him while she tried to find out if he had seen someone in the garden.

"Your mother and Antonia are playing cards," she remarked for want of anything else to say.

He nodded. She sensed he was still waiting.

Molly wandered over to the fireplace and ran her fingers over a pretty ormulu clock ticking softly. "This is very nice."

"Thank you." After a moment, he asked, "Is something wrong, Miss Mills?"

"No. Nothing." She looked over to see him

148

watching her. Molly circled around to the windows and looked out into the courtyard. It was empty. "Perhaps a turn about the courtyard would be nice," she mused aloud.

"It is chilly outside."

"It is not so cold as all that. Sometimes people even walk in the rain," she noted without looking at him.

"I think one would have to be worried or very lonely to go out into the rain." Through the panes of glass, she watched his reflection and saw him put down his drawing pen. "Are you lonely, Miss Mills?" he asked in a softer voice than she had ever heard him use.

"Why would you think that?"

"It would not be surprising. After all, you are far away from your home and from most of your family."

She turned back to him. "That is true." The conversation was not following the path she had intended, yet instead of trying to turn it back, she found herself asking him, "Do you ever get lonely?"

"My work keeps me busy."

"Work is scarcely a substitute for companionship."

"Men are different from women. Men do not need to be constantly in the company of others."

"I do not think men are different from women at all," she retorted.

A smile licked at his mouth. "No? I do not think I would wear that dress nearly as well as you."

She reddened slightly and acknowledged, "Well, yes, in some ways they are different. That is, men and women may be shaped differently, but when it comes to companionship, everyone feels the same

149

need for it." He really must think her wits had gone begging to stand here talking about the differences between men and women and about loneliness. Yet she could not ask outright if he had seen a figure walking in the rain and if, by chance, that figure was her uncle Brace, who might be lying to her. Deceit seemed the only acceptable course for her. Only, Molly recalled, she had never been very good at lying.

"Are you certain there is nothing wrong, Molly?"

She was surprised by the use of her given name. She made a small gesture with her hands and tried for a half-truth. "Antonia thought she saw a ghost walking in the garden in the rain. Since you have a door that opens onto the courtyard, I thought it might have been you. If it was you, I thought you might be troubled or unhappy. I—I wanted to make certain everything was well with you."

"That is very kind."

Indeed, she thought he seemed touched. "I know you have been working hard on the plans for the prince, and then you had to track all over England to find your possessions after the gypsy took them." Not to mention—which she did not—his unexpected guests. She tried for a laugh. "You are probably wishing yourself back in London."

He remained serious, almost reflective. "It's very peaceful here. London can be amusing, but one seldom has a chance to take a brisk ride and feel the air or to visit with tenants. I have had little chance to do so this visit, but I like to sit down with the simple people who live close to the earth."

Molly had never heard him sound so philosophical. Somehow, though, the conversation was becoming too intimate, and she wanted to change that.

"You have not even mentioned that we have been alone for fifteen minutes without a chaperon and that we are trouncing upon the rules of polite society."

"You seem to think little enough of those rules," he noted. "They do have a purpose, you know."

"To teach young ladies that gentlemen are untrustworthy?" she asked prettily. "Should I feel unsafe with you?"

She expected a quick retort. Instead, he remained silent and watched her with an inscrutable expression.

Molly recalled what he had said earlier about the differences between a man and a woman. He had also kissed her. Not that she had objected or that she looked back with regret. On the contrary, there had been something exciting, even breathless, about that moment.

"I do not even know the sort of life you are used to back in Ireland," he said, breaking the silence. "Do you go to dances and soirees?"

"Of course. I am not without some accomplishments," she added a touch defiantly.

"I am sure you are not."

"Although," she confided, "I do not play the pianoforte as well as either of my sisters. I daresay by English standards I am sadly lacking."

"There are more important things than playing the pianoforte well."

She did not ask what those other things were. Already the discussion had become more personal than she had intended. It was time, she decided, to leave. Smiling vaguely, Molly gathered up her skirts. "I am sorry I disturbed your work. I must make certain Antonia is all right."

"Didn't you say she is with my mother?"

"Yes." She laughed. "That is why I must look in upon them."

He smiled back at her. "They are serious about their cards. I hope they have not done each other an injury."

His smile was engaging, and she almost wished she could think of some other subject of conversation that would allow her to remain. But she could think of nothing else to say, so she started toward the door.

Chapter 9

MOLLY HAD not been back with Antonia and Lady Lindworth above ten minutes when the door swung open and a flushed-looking maid rushed in. "Begging your pardon, milady, but a lady and a gentleman are here."

Lady Lindworth looked up. "In this weather?"

"Yes, milady."

"Did they present calling cards?"

"No. They came in a hired coach and are just now having their luggage unloaded. I believe they mean to stay."

Lady Lindworth rose and said faintly, "Send for my son immediately."

The maid rushed away.

Molly put her book aside and watched with unabashed interest. This promised to be exciting.

The dowager stared haughtily down at Antonia. "I shall be gone a short time. Do not look at my cards."

Antonia tossed back her mane of hair. "Of course not."

Lady Lindworth was halfway out of the room when Molly heard a familiar woman's voice trill, "Such a delightful house."

A moment later Mrs. Wiley appeared in the doorway. She wore a shocking purple gown. A lavender shawl was flung about her shoulders, and a peacock-feathered purple hat sat askew on her bright blond curls. She beamed at Molly and Antonia as if they were long-lost daughters.

But it was not the sight of Mrs. Wiley that caused Molly to rise in stunned disbelief. Beside Mrs. Wiley stood Daniel Ryan. Daniel, who was Molly's Irish swain and the man she had not expected to see for several weeks. Daniel of the thick brown hair and booming brogue. He stood in the doorway looking hearty and robust as he smiled to one and all. When he saw her, he rushed forward and swept her into an unceremonious hug.

"Devilish appealing gown, Moll," he whispered into her ear.

Molly could only stare speechlessly. Over his shoulder, she saw a panic-stricken Lady Lindworth. Then Lord Lindworth appeared beside his mother.

The dowager crumpled into a chair.

The earl stepped forward toward Daniel. "May I say your arrival is unexpected. I do not believe we have had the pleasure of meeting."

Daniel kept an arm around Molly. "I am Daniel Ryan. Miss Mills is my betrothed."

That was news to Molly since he had never actually proposed. She blinked up at him.

"I came to England to see her and discovered she was no longer in Bath. One of the servants told me she was headed northward to deliver furniture purchased from Mrs. Wiley. I immediately contacted Mrs. Wiley. She was overcome with concern for me and insisted on accompanying me here." He beamed down at Molly and squeezed her shoulder.

"Oh, dear," Lady Lindworth whimpered.

154

Lord Lindworth hesitated, clearly uncertain how to handle the uninvited friends of uninvited guests.

"Didn't mean to intrude on you like this, but we stopped at the inn and met your brother there."

"Henry," Antonia put in brightly.

"Yes, that's the one," Daniel agreed, as if there might be legions of brothers. "He wouldn't hear of us taking a room. Insisted we come up here and present ourselves tonight, so here we are," he finished happily.

Mrs. Wiley stepped forward with a pretty little speech. "We are so delighted to be here after our long and arduous journey. It was too bad of us to not send word, I know, but I knew you were not the sort to stand on ceremony." Mrs. Wiley turned to address herself to Lady Lindworth. "Such an enchanting house. I was so pleased I could assist in reuniting you with your furniture. I treated everything as if it were the king's own furnishings," Mrs. Wiley continued. "Naturally, I knew at a glance it came from one of the finest homes in England."

Molly hid a smile as she recalled the sight of the priceless furniture stacked unceremoniously in Mrs. Wiley's spare room. She also suspected Mrs. Wiley's motives for wanting to accompany Daniel were not so pure as she would have everyone believe. Mrs. Wiley still cast an appraising eye about at the furnishings and would doubtless use any opportunity to benefit from this journey.

"Naturally, you are welcome to stay here," the earl said. Molly almost felt sorry for him. She suspected he would ring a peal over Henry's head when next he saw him. For now, though, there was little else he could do.

"Damned hospitable of you, Lindworth. 'M pleased to accept. We came through a bad storm."

"A dreadful storm," Mrs. Wiley echoed. "We would have stopped hours ago, but Daniel was so anxious to reach his betrothed. I find that dreadfully romantic, don't you?" she asked the room at large.

"Dreadfully." Lady Lindworth looked faint.

Lord Lindworth made no reply.

"Of course, this storm was nothing to Daniel after having braved the Irish Sea to reach his beloved." Mrs. Wiley dabbed at her eyes with the lace edge of her handkerchief. "I am overcome with the sheer emotion of such devotion."

"The sea was a wee bit of a rough go," Daniel agreed, and beamed down at Molly. "I won't have to brave it alone when I go back, though."

"You might," Antonia put in. "Molly may never return if it means getting deathly ill again."

Molly knew she should have been excited by Daniel's arrival. At the very least, she ought to feel happy. At the moment, however, she felt uneasy. It might have been the rigid way the earl held himself, or it might have been Mrs. Wiley's exuberant grin that caused her reaction.

Lord Lindworth stepped toward the bellpull and rang for the servants. "You must be tired. I shall have you shown to your rooms."

Mrs. Wiley flitted out, and Daniel left after a final lingering look back at Molly. Lady Lindworth's abigail was summoned to assist her ladyship upstairs to her rooms. Antonia darted out after the guests to see if Daniel had brought her any presents.

That left Molly and Lord Lindworth alone in the drawing room.

"You seem to be acquiring company rapidly." Molly did not look above the level of the knot in his cravat. She seldom felt so uncertain, even guilty.

"I confess I was surprised to find a man declaring his intentions for you. In light of this, some of my actions toward you seem even more inappropriate."

He was thinking of the stolen kiss, she supposed.

"Daniel will return to Ireland before long. We will all be leaving," she added, then laughed ruefully. "I daresay that is beginning to sound like an empty promise to you. It is only that my uncle's health has not improved, and we cannot leave until it does."

"Of course," he said stiffly.

Why did she feel so ill at ease? It was not as if Daniel's presence changed anything between herself and Lord Lindworth. At best they had been acquaintances. Certainly they had not formed any sort of attachment toward each other.

Somewhere in the distance, she heard Mrs. Wiley exclaiming, "This is the perfect spot for the jardiniere. Is this English ivy planted in it? What a positively superb choice. So simple yet so splendid."

Molly could not repress a smile.

"I should not be surprised if it did not fetch a goodly sum at auction," Mrs. Wiley continued.

The earl paled, and Molly's smile faded. "I fear Mrs. Wiley is accustomed to thinking of furniture in terms of its value."

"The furniture is not for sale," he said stiffly.

"Yes, of course." But if the earl thought to dampen the irrepressible Mrs. Wiley, Molly thought he would face a challenge. "I had better go look in on Antonia."

Turning, Molly hurried out of the room. For once, she agreed with the rule they not be alone in a room together. She was anxious to escape so that she did not have to look into those piercing gray eyes and wonder what he was thinking and feeling. Neither did she want to measure her own thoughts and feelings toward him. It was better to leave.

"It only gets worse and worse," Lady Lindworth moaned from the settee by the window in her room. She lay with her hands crossed martyrlike over her bosom. Now and again, she sighed pathetically. A maid hovered nearby.

It was the morning after the guests' arrival, and Lord Lindworth was out of temper himself. He had not slept well last night, distracted as he was with berouged women and Irish suitors.

"Mother, do not overset yourself. Within a day or so they will be gone."

"How do you know the prince will not arrive before then? He is already late." Lady Lindworth showed more spirit than Lawrence had seen in some time. "Did you see that woman turning the vases over and looking for imprints? I should not be surprised if she and the gypsy are not in league with each other. They may strip the house again. Oh, dear, I feel quite faint." The maid hurried forward to apply warm towels to her ladyship's forehead.

"And Mr. Ryan! He is deplorable. Miss Mills is a comely girl, so it is not surprising that she is engaged. But for Mr. Ryan to come seeking her without even sending notice to us. Really, Lawrence, it is more than I can bear."

At that moment, Henry sauntered into the room. Lady Lindworth intoned weakly, "There is the son who wishes to see me in my coffin."

"What talk is this?" Henry demanded heartily.

Lady Lindworth gathered the strength to rise up on her elbows. "You sent those dreadful people to stay with us and then you disappeared for the whole of a day. It is bad enough that we have to endure Miss Mills and her cousin. By the by, the child has not the least notion how to play cards. It is only luck when she wins. Luck and nothing more."

Henry crossed the room and dropped a kiss on his mother's cheek. "It is not so bad as all that. Miss Mills is charming, and Antonia is becoming quite a good shot with the bow and arrow."

"Miss Mills is Irish. Oh, I'll own she has a pretty face and a pleasant enough disposition. If she were taken under someone's wing, she might be turned into someone who could give a good account of herself. But that is beside the point of Mr. Ryan."

"Well, I should not worry about him. He and Molly will spend most of their time exploring the estate and gazing into each other's eyes. Why, I saw them walking out not ten minutes ago."

"Unchaperoned?" Lady Lindworth asked in horror.

"No, Antonia was with them, and a maid and a dog. I should not think it very romantic to have so many trailing along."

Lord Lindworth threw himself into a wing chair and studied his brother. He wondered what Henry knew of romance or the way two people could feel toward each other.

"Where were you?" Lady Lindworth asked plaintively.

"Conducting business."

There was no mention of a horse. Lawrence studied his brother. He had not noticed until now how excessively cheerful and satisfied with himself Henry looked. That worried Lawrence.

"Mrs. Wiley is downstairs inspecting the furniture in the gallery," Henry reported.

Lady Lindworth sighed. "What will she do next?"

"Besides flirting with the footman?" Henry asked innocently.

"She isn't!"

"Well, James does not seem to object. He was flirting back."

"That woman is without shame. Lawrence, you must do something."

Yes, it appeared he must.

"Oh, I have a bit of other news." Henry grinned. "The Prince Regent will be here in two days."

"Hartshorn, Lawrence. Quickly."

Molly stepped over a small boulder and continued up the incline. She and Daniel were headed back to the house after a walk through meadows dotted with white sheep. It was a pleasant day of blue-green skies and refreshing breezes. Daniel walked beside her through the long grass, and now and again touched her arm. She smiled up at him.

The dog bounded ahead, and Antonia ran alongside him.

Daniel thumped his hand-carved walking stick firmly into the ground with each step. "It is a pretty enough place even if it is not Ireland."

"It is pleasant," Molly agreed. She had come to feel quite at home with the countryside around the estate.

"Of course, I know you pine to return home."

Did she? Yes, of course she must. "Yes."

He glanced at her and cleared his throat. "I know I spoke hastily the other night when I said we were engaged to be wed. I have never formally proposed to you, and I have not even applied to your uncle for your hand."

Molly kept her eyes averted demurely downward. She and Daniel had known each other since they were in leading strings. He would be a good and steady husband. Marrying him would surely be the right thing to do. She was not a fanciful young girl, but she did want him to ask her to marry him in a romantic fashion.

"You are not saying anything, Molly."

She gazed up at him. "I was surprised, but I am not angry. I did think, though, that you would speak to me privately later." She wanted only a few endearments and a few promises of future happiness. Not that she hesitated about marrying him; certainly she did not.

"Well, no need for that now." Daniel seemed to believe the subject was finished, and he proceeded to talk about the healthy coat on the dog.

Molly felt the fledgling stirring of exasperation. When Daniel moved on to talk about the dog's teeth, she interrupted, "When will we marry?"

"When?" He looked at her as if the question had not occurred to him. "Oh, whenever you wish. Well, not the week of the hunt. I should not want to miss the excitement of leaping slurried ditches and riding down hairy banks."

Molly stared at him. "You would let a hunt determine the date of the wedding?"

He pulled her to a stop beside him and looked

down at her with concern. "Ah, I see how it is. You are no longer a green girl, and you want the wedding to take place as soon as possible."

"I do not consider myself old," Molly told him crossly.

"No, you are not on the shelf, but time is adding up. If you wish, we could be married here by special license. We might even be able to get the earl to marry us." He peered intently into her face. "Why did you turn pale?"

"I would like to go back to the house now, Daniel. I am suddenly tired." She was also possessed of the desire to be away from her beloved. Quickly.

"I never knew you to feel tired before, Molly. This English weather cannot be good for you. It is not good for your uncle, either. Look how it has affected his health."

Since that subject had come up, what *was* the state of her uncle's health? "How did you think Uncle Brace looked?" she asked.

Daniel shrugged and whistled for the dog. "He said he ached all over."

"But how did you think he looked?" Molly pressed.

"Like a man who has been too long in England."

She sighed. Clearly she was not getting anywhere.

Antonia danced back toward them with the dog at her side. "Why did you stop walking?"

"We were talking," Molly told her. "We are coming now."

"Well, hurry. Henry is back, and he is going to show me how to make the arrow go into a high arc when I shoot."

"I should like to learn that myself," Daniel said,

162

and patted the dog's head. The frisky animal leaped around and nearly knocked Molly off her feet.

Daniel steadied her with strong hands. As they started back toward the house, he observed, "Henry seems a good man. I suppose the earl is, too, but he is dull."

"He is kind to his tenants," Molly said.

"A lot of kind people are dull."

"The earl is not dull. He is interested in architecture and he is very clever at creating plans."

Daniel yawned.

That annoyed Molly. She thought Lord Lindworth's efforts were admirable, especially since many men in his position did nothing save gamble and amuse themselves with women. She was about to flare up at Daniel when she reminded herself that he had come across the sea to be with her. It was foolish to argue about someone who was of no real consequence in their lives. Once they left here, they would never see the earl again.

Dinner that evening was elegant but strained. Lawrence was surprised that his mother joined the guests. It was true she looked wan and fluttery, but she was present. She had sent him a desperate note that afternoon begging him to speak to Mrs. Wiley and Mr. Ryan and convince them to leave.

Mrs. Wiley was dressed like a peacock in a bright blue gown with lavender bows around a neck that dipped low, and a red feather fan that she swished incessantly. Feathers were falling off and floating about. From where Lawrence sat at the head of the table, he saw Henry trying to fish one out of his wineglass.

For some reason, Henry had invited Lord Norton

to dinner. Lawrence was glad he was here; he felt in need of someone to talk to. Lord Norton sat across from Mrs. Wiley, watching her with rapt attention. Seated beside Mrs. Wiley, Miss Mills looked positively demure in a pretty pink gown. She also seemed subdued. Her cousin did not join them for the meal, having announced earlier that she was dining with her father.

"The ragout is simply excellent, Lady Lindworth. You must give me the receipt." Without waiting for a response, Mrs. Wiley turned her attention across the table to Lord Norton. "Do you have an estate nearby?"

"Yes, Woodsmere."

"What a wonderful name. Woodsmere. I am certain it is full of the finest antiques and furnishings." She lowered her voice to confide, "I am available to appraise furniture should you ever find yourself in need of funds."

Henry made a choking noise and disappeared behind his damask napkin, whence could be heard muffled laughter.

Lawrence was not amused.

Lord Norton shook his head politely. "I do not believe I shall need your services."

She lifted bare shoulders in an insouciant shrug. "Should you change your mind, I am not hard to find."

"Indeed, Mrs. Wiley is easy to locate," Daniel agreed cheerfully. "I came all the way from Ireland and had no trouble finding her."

" 'Tis true." Mrs. Wiley adjusted one of the lavender bows on her gown and fluttered a smile around the table. "Mr. Ryan appeared on my doorstep after having learned what a dear, dear friend

I am to little Antonia and sweet Molly. I knew instantly that he was a man in love, and I saw it as my duty to help reunite him with the woman of his heart."

The earl ran his finger along the edge of his knife and wondered if everyone else found Mrs. Wiley's tale as irritating as he did.

"At any rate," she continued, still stroking the bow, "I could do nothing less than accompany him here. He was, after all, a stranger in our land and in need of guidance. Anyone who knows me knows I am helpful to a fault. So we came here." She ended with a beatific smile.

"Well, I did pay you," Daniel reminded her.

Her smile flickered, then resumed its brightness. "A pittance. I would have been glad to help reunite you without even a sou. You must know that. I am not a woman driven by money."

No one contradicted her aloud.

The earl's glance skimmed down the table to Miss Mills. She was quieter than usual. Was she happy to be sitting across from her betrothed? Yes, of course she must be, but it was hard to tell by her impassive expression. Then she turned her head, and the candles caught at her lustrous hair and her eyes twinkled, and she looked suddenly very beguiling. Why had he thought that she would be anything less than delighted to be with the man she was to wed? What startled him was how hollow—even sad—he felt at seeing Molly Mills with another man.

After dinner, the ladies repaired to the drawing room, and the men remained over port. It was a strained affair, and they did not linger long before joining the ladies. While Daniel went immediately to Molly, Lady Lindworth continued her card play with Antonia. Mrs. Wiley and Henry were engaged in some conversation when Lawrence drew Lord Norton out onto the cool balcony.

"I find myself in an awkward situation," Lawrence began without preliminaries.

The marquis gave a knowing wink. "I can see that. Your new guests are hardly the sort one wishes to have in his home when the Prince Regent comes to visit. If you can rid yourself of Mrs. Wiley and that Ryan fellow, the others are not so bad."

"I cannot ask Mr. Ryan to leave. He is Miss Mills's betrothed."

"What has that to say to anything?"

"It would hurt her if I asked him to leave."

Lord Norton looked at him quizzically. Slowly a light came on in his eyes. "Ah, I see how it is. You have developed a *tendre* for her."

"Of course not. But I have come to respect her, and I would not like to see her unhappy."

The marquis inclined his head toward Lawrence's mother. "What does Lady Lindworth say?"

Lawrence chuckled sadly. "You would not want to know."

"I expect I already do. They can stay at the inn, you know."

Yes, he knew that. It was a practical solution, but it did not take into account how Molly would feel. Why he should concern himself with her feelings was a mystery. The important thing was the impression he and his household made on the Prince Regent. Wasn't it?

His friend clapped him on the shoulder. "You are in a coil, Lawrence. Must say I never thought to see you in a situation like this. You're always so proper and dignified, and you don't allow yourself to become encumbered with people like this. I'd like to stay and help you sort it out, but I must get back. My best mare is having a foal tonight, and I want to be there."

Norton made a cheerful exit, leaving Lawrence alone on the balcony.

He was not to remain there long before Daniel appeared in the doorway. "Don't mean to disturb you, but this will only take a moment." He closed the door behind him. "May I speak to you bluntly?"

Daniel Ryan was the last person in the realm Lawrence wanted to speak with.

"It's about Molly. Seems she is more anxious to wed than I had realized. I had intended to wait until we returned to Ireland, but she wants to marry quickly." He lifted his hands in a vague gesture. "Well, she *is* on the shelf. On her next birthday, she will be one-and-twenty. It stands to reason she would be eager to marry."

"I had never gained the impression marriage was an urgent matter with her. She had never mentioned you," the earl added meanly.

Daniel took no offense. Grinning, he said, "Molly can keep her secrets when she wants to. It's one of the things I like about Moll."

"What is it you want of me?" Lawrence asked without any false cover of pleasantness.

"I wondered if a ceremony could be arranged here within the next day or so. You must know the vicar or whoever would perform a wedding."

It was all the earl could do to keep a civil tongue in his head. "Mr. Ryan, I am expecting royalty in my home," he said sharply. "This is not the time

167

to arrange a marriage ceremony here." Even if he had been so inclined.

"Moll will be disappointed."

"Then she will just have to be," Lawrence snapped.

Daniel looked at him curiously. "I must own, I thought you would be more helpful, especially since Molly said she has been assisting you. Seems a bit ungrateful of you."

Lawrence could not remember the last time he had felt such an urge to thrash a man. He was a gentle employer and had never raised a hand to anyone who worked for him. Yes, he had frequented Gentleman Jackson's in London, but never with the intention of beating someone senseless. Yet that idea held great charm for him at the moment. He had to make an effort to restrain himself.

"I cannot help you," he said coldly.

Daniel sighed. "I do not suppose you would tell Molly that? I have a difficult time being the bearer of bad news."

"No, I will not tell her. If there is nothing further you wish to discuss, I am going to retire now." Without waiting for a reply, he turned and stalked away. He was not often so rude, but he was seldom so provoked.

Chapter 10

THE NEXT day Molly and Daniel strolled in the garden. He picked flowers of gold and purple for her, and he made her laugh with his stories about their friends back in Ireland.

Afterward he tried his hand with the bow and arrow and shrugged easily when he hit wide of the mark. He laughed when Antonia teased him. Daniel was as genial as ever. Any woman would count herself fortunate to have him as a husband, Molly told herself as she stepped up to try shooting the bow. Yet she was aware of a new reluctance.

Her arrow soared through the air, only to drop short of the target.

She moved back to join Daniel. "We are neither one very good."

"No," he agreed, and watched Antonia. "I saw your uncle this morning. He still wants to introduce our Antonia into English society."

"Yes, I know." Molly examined the grass at her feet. It was still slightly damp from the dew, and here and there a drop of water glistened in the sunlight. "I fear Uncle is going to be very disappointed."

Daniel cleared his throat. "Moll, since we are

speaking of disappointments, I also have some bad news."

She waited for him to continue. When he did not, she prompted, "Yes?"

He looked at her sheepishly. "You know I have never liked to give anyone unhappy news."

"I know." She also knew unless she prompted him, he would talk in convoluted sentences for half an hour before she dragged anything out of him. "Just say it straightaway, Daniel, and be done with it."

He inhaled a deep breath. "I spoke with the earl last night. It did not seem to me he wanted to be helpful, Moll. It's true one cannot always—"

"Daniel," she urged.

"He cannot help us wed."

Her lashes came down in a long, slow blink. Why had Daniel gone to Lord Lindworth with such an outrageous request in the first place?

"I told him you wished to be married quickly, and I asked for his assistance in hurrying matters along."

"You didn't!"

Antonia shouted, "I hit it! I hit the center of the target."

"That's wonderful, lass," Daniel called, then turned anxiously back to Molly. "Don't be angry, Moll."

"Angry? I am mortified."

"I reminded him you had helped with his work, and I said it was dashed uncivil of him to refuse to help."

Molly looked up into Daniel's earnest face and shook her head hopelessly. "You don't understand." How could she explain when she was not certain she understood herself? But the earl was the last person she wanted Daniel to speak to.

"We can get married in Ireland," Daniel said in a comforting voice. "Not during hunting season, though."

"First you go to Lord Lindworth and try to arrange a hurried marriage, and now you are saying you may not be available for the ceremony at certain times of the year." Molly tried to keep the bite of sarcasm out of her words, but did not succeed.

Daniel looked wounded. "Moll, you've always been a woman of understanding. Surely you know how it is with a man and his bloodhounds and the foxes."

"I am not certain I do. In fact, I have always regarded that as a barbaric sport."

He gazed at her as if she were a stranger, then shook his head sadly. "Very well, we shall wed whenever you say, even if it is during the height of the hunt." He spoke in long-suffering accent.

Impatiently she said, "That is not the point."

He heaved a frustrated sigh. "I don't know what you want from me. I am trying to be as agreeable as possible."

Henry's return was a welcome distraction. He galloped into the meadow, slid from his horse, and beamed around triumphantly. He had a fine coating of dust as if he had ridden some distance, and his cravat was unraveling into a tired linen wreck.

Antonia rushed over, abandoning her bow and quiver of arrows on the grass. "Did you have good luck?"

"Splendid. Everything is going to work out exactly as we planned." He threw his head back and laughed with glee. "The bait has been taken, if you understand my meaning."

Daniel turned a confused face to Molly. "What is he talking about?"

"I shall explain later." She retied the strings of her pert red bonnet and smoothed the skirts of her gray striped day dress. Instead of listening to Henry's excited words, she thought about the conversation that must have taken place between Daniel and the earl. She felt humiliated. The earl must think she was desperate to wed. How was she going to face him again? She knew one thing for certain: this visit had gone on long enough.

Henry was still talking when Molly abruptly excused herself and went to see her uncle.

He looked up with a broad smile from his chair by the window when she entered. "I saw you riding across the field with Daniel. You make a handsome couple."

She did not respond to that. "How do you feel?" she asked directly.

Uncle Brace leaned back in his chair, and his smile deepened in his florid face. "I feel much better. I should not be surprised if I am not completely recovered within the next day or so."

"The Prince Regent arrives tomorrow."

"What a coincidence. I shall probably be strong enough to meet him."

"Uncle Brace, if you are better tomorrow, it is time we left." In light of what Daniel had just told her, the sooner she was away from here, the better. She did not want the earl looking at her with pity.

His smile died. "I am not feeling that strong, child."

Molly leaned toward him in an effort to convey

he urgency of her request. "We can go back to
Bath, and you can take the waters there. It might
be just what you need to cure you."

"I am perfectly happy to take the waters, but we
cannot go until I am well enough to travel." He
stared at her resentfully, as if she were without
feeling to suggest such a thing. "Surely you would
not ask that of me."

She bit back a sigh. "No, Uncle."

He softened. "You have my promise we will be
gone within the week. You're a good girl, Molly,
and I don't want to distress you further. Tomorrow
we shall lay firm plans for our departure."

It was the most definite thing she had heard him
say. Hearing it should have calmed her. Yet as she
left the room and wandered the halls, she felt as
tightly wound as a coil.

Lord Lindworth paced about the little courtyard
for some time before the answer presented itself.
The solution was so obvious, he wondered that it
had not come to him before now. Mrs. Wiley's suggestion to Lord Norton that she was available to
appraise furnishings was the key.

The earl had always been honest in his dealings
with others, and he disliked the thought of prevar-
ication. Yet circumstances demanded action, and
the only way he could think to accomplish that was
with lies. He might as well do it and be done with
it, he decided, and started back into the house in
search of Mrs. Wiley.

Lawrence found her in the library examining the
books there. She greeted him with a wide, red smile.
"You have some valuable tomes, milord. Did you
know that?"

"Yes, they have been in the family for generations."

"It is time the rest of the world had the opportunity to appreciate them. At auction they would draw a pretty sum. A very pretty sum."

He wanted to tell her that nothing from this estate would ever go to auction. He wanted to say that good breeding dictated she not put a price on everything in the house. But that, Lawrence told himself, would defeat the reason he had sought her out. He tilted his head to the side and manufactured a look of interest. "Really?"

"Oh, yes." Mrs. Wiley's smile brightened. "Of course, you would want someone to represent you in any such transaction. I would be willing to do so."

Of course she would, Lawrence thought dryly. "Mrs. Wiley, my mother would never consent to selling any of the books from the library. However . . ." He lowered his voice confidentially, causing her to lean forward aggressively, in the process revealing not a small amount of bosom spilling forth from her daring jade green gown. "However, Mrs. Wiley, I am not opposed to considering selling some of my own property."

She blinked in surprise.

He looked down toward the floor. "I find myself in a rather delicate situation regarding funds."

"Yes?" She bent forward, eager to hear more.

"At my house in London I have some rare books and some antiques that might fetch a high price. You know the sort of thing," he added casually, "a Roman goblet with a few gems in it. A sword from the Crusades. That sort of thing."

She was wide-eyed and breathless. "Do you want to sell them?"

"Only if it can be done discreetly."

"I am the soul of discretion," she whispered.

The red on her mouth strayed outside the bounds of her lips, he noted as he leaned closer to ask in a low voice, "Would it be possible for you to go to London and appraise some of my possessions? I shall, of course, put my carriage at your disposal for the journey. I do not mean to press the matter, but it would be most helpful if you could go tomorrow."

"Tomorrow?" Her enthusiasm dimmed visibly. "The prince arrives tomorrow."

"Yes." Lawrence feigned a look of regret. "But I must raise funds right away. A gambling debt, you see. Very pressing. Well, I don't want to bore you with the particulars of my problems, but if you are not free to go, I daresay I can find someone in London to arrange everything."

Her brows drew together, and she gnawed at her lower lip. She was plainly torn between greed and a desire to look into the face of royalty. Greed carried the day. She nodded decisively. "I shall go."

"Splendid. I shall have the carriage ready to leave at first light."

"Gracious, you are in a rush."

He shrugged helplessly. "I gambled deeply and am sorely pressed."

"I understand. I shall not tell the first person."

As Mrs. Wiley flitted out of the room, he suspected his gambling debts would be the talk of London before she had been in that city an hour. He did not care. He had other matters to consider. The first was to pen a letter to his butler in London telling him not to allow Mrs. Wiley into the house under any circumstances. Lawrence also enclosed a handsome sum to be given to Mrs. Wiley to soften the blow as she continued on to Bath. He sealed the envelope, went out to the stables, and soon had a man riding toward London.

That task completed, the earl sought out his panic-stricken mother. He found her in her little sitting room with the pretty yellow flowers painted on the walls.

"Mrs. Wiley is leaving in the morning," he announced.

Lady Lindworth burst into a tremulous smile. "You are a saint, Lawrence."

"There are people who would argue that," he noted skeptically. Molly Mills for one.

"Is Mr. Ryan leaving as well?"

"No, I am afraid we shall just have to endure him. And Sir Brace as well. We can do nothing but wait for his health to improve."

His mother sighed.

"I have done the best I could."

"You are a good son," his mother murmured.

He smiled ruefully at the realization he was no longer a saint.

"As long as our guests remain, you might as well send little Miss Antonia to my room. Tell her to bring the playing cards," her ladyship added as he rose to leave.

"Yes, Mother."

As he started out into the hall, the earl thought his most challenging confrontations were over. He soon discovered they were not.

He should have realized that the moment he saw Daniel Ryan approaching him in the hall.

"I must speak with you," the Irishman said.

Another plea to arrange a quick marriage? Lawrence ran tired hands through his hair. "We can talk in my study."

Their footsteps sounded loud and ominous as they trooped down the hall. Once in his study, the earl offered his guest a seat and sat down behind his own desk.

Daniel sat but immediately bounded to his feet again. "I am a man of my word, Lawrence. You don't object to me using your given name, I hope." Daniel Ryan went on without waiting for a reply. "I am also a gentleman. Oh, I know I may not have all the trappings as you, but I own land and I am highly respected in Ireland."

"Mr. Ryan, I am afraid I do not see how this—"

"I came to England with the best of intentions. Molly, as you must know, is a wonderful woman. Pretty as a picture with her silken hair flying and her green eyes dancing. Winsome in every way, don't you agree?"

Lord Lindworth hesitated, recalling the sight of Molly with the candlelight playing into her eyes, and her cheeks pink as rose blossoms.

"Not that she is without fault, you understand. She rides badly and she cannot handle the reins. I have seen her overturn a pony cart."

Why was the man here telling him this? "Mr. Ryan, I do not know what you want."

Daniel pivoted on his right foot and looked the earl squarely in the eye. "I like Molly. I do not mean to hurt her."

Lawrence's fingers closed around his chair arm.

"She's a strong lass and not given to hysterics,

177

but I cannot say how she might act when she dis covers the truth."

Lawrence felt a slow anger rising. What was this man about to do to Molly? If Daniel Ryan hurt her Lawrence would call him out himself.

"I like her a great deal, but I do not want to marry her," Daniel blurted.

The room was suddenly silent. Except for the clock ticking on the mantel, the only sound was the men's breathing.

"What did you say?" Lawrence asked slowly.

"I came here with the best of intentions. We have known each other since we were children. But she has changed. She does not understand about the hunt. She is pressing too hard for marriage. The truth is, I no longer know if I am in love with her."

The earl cleared his throat uncomfortably. Love was not necessary for a match. At least the earl had always believed that. Yet he understood something of what this strange Irishman was saying. "Mr. Ryan, I think you and Miss Mills should discuss this together."

Daniel stopped in midstep and bent his head. "I can't. I have never been good at telling people bad news. How can I tell her I no longer wish to marry her when poor Molly wanted to set a date the moment I arrived? It will devastate her if I cry off."

Lawrence had listened to the confidences of confused men before. He had heard the woes of men in love with actresses, and men who wished to shed mistresses who clung to them. In short, Lawrence had heard everything, but he had never been as perplexed about how to proceed as he was now. The truth was, he would be glad if Daniel did not marry Miss Mills. It was that simple.

Daniel spread his hands in a plea for help. "Moll is a good sort, and it would cut me up to see her in tears." He looked back down at the floor. "I cannot do it. I am leaving tomorrow. Mrs. Wiley has arranged to have a carriage at her disposal, and I will journey south with her. You must tell Molly for me that I have left and that I will not be returning."

Lawrence wanted to shake Daniel. It was Daniel's place to give such news. Mostly, though, he wanted this damned Irishman to go away.

Rising abruptly, the earl said, "If I refuse, what will happen?"

Daniel sighed. "I will write Molly a letter once I return to Ireland and tell her how it must be."

Coward. The earl rose and stalked about the room. "You are behaving in a shameless fashion."

Daniel had the grace to look guilty.

"It will only embarrass her more to hear the news from me."

Daniel shook his head. "I do not think so. She likes you. She has praised you to me. Besides, you are an earl. You have the breeding to say things in just the right way. You can frame the words to make her understand it is for the best. Molly would not want a reluctant bridegroom. What woman would?"

The earl wondered why Molly had ever wanted this man in the first place. Yes, she was twenty years old, but with her beauty and her spirit, she still could make a match with someone honest enough to speak plainly with her.

Daniel reached the door and turned the handle. "If I do not see you again before I leave, thank you for your hospitality."

He was gone.

Curiously, Molly noted that Daniel did not com
to dinner. She also noted that the conversatio
seemed tense and there was a sense of strain in th
air. After dinner, Molly was ready to flee. She ex
cused herself and started for the door, but the ear
stopped her.

"I wondered if I could prevail upon you to hel
me finish a few details on the sketches for tomor
row."

Finish details? She had heard him tell his mothe
at dinner that everything was in readiness for th
visit. Still, it was easier to agree to do as he aske
than to argue.

"I should be glad to help. I shall collect my mai
for a chaperon and come down in a few minutes."

"Your maid is not necessary."

She stared speechlessly.

The earl looked everywhere except at her.

"Very well." She allowed him to escort her down
to his study, where she found all the drawings
neatly stacked on his desk. "What do you want me
to do?"

He guided her toward a chair and sat down across
from her. "Nothing."

When she started to rise, he pushed her gently
back down.

"I lied to draw you down here so I could speak
with you alone." Before she could frame a reply, he
rushed on, "Miss Mills, this is not easy for me to
say. You are a charming young woman, and men
seek you out. But sometimes men change their
minds about the way they feel."

He paused to look at her, and she met his gaze

silently. For a moment, something flickered deep in his eyes, and then it was gone.

"Please tell me what you are saying, milord."

He sighed. "Daniel is leaving in the morning."

Molly rose in agitation. "I cannot possibly be ready to go by then." This did not make any sense. Why hadn't Daniel told her? What about Uncle Brace and Antonia?

He reached for her hand. "He does not want you to go with him."

She froze.

"He is going back to Ireland without you, Molly. He no longer wishes to marry you."

A dozen different emotions raced through her. She felt anger and surprise and confusion. She felt embarrassment and uncertainty. Most of all, though, she felt relieved.

"I am sorry to have to tell you this," he said quietly.

She could find no words for her jumbled thoughts. How must this look to the earl? Proud, haughty Molly Mills had been abandoned by the man who had come all the way from Ireland to say he wanted to marry her. Worse, Daniel had left the task of telling her of his abandonment to Lord Lindworth.

She should be grieving over the end of her engagement and the death of her plans for a future with Daniel. She should cry, shouldn't she? Yet tears did not spring to her eyes.

"Should I ring for your maid?" he asked.

She shook her head.

"This does not mean you are undesirable," he told her gently. "Because two people do not suit does not suggest there is anything wrong with either of

181

them. Certainly there is nothing about you with which to find fault."

Molly had heard enough. Her humiliation was complete enough without his trumped-up compliments. Drawing herself up proudly, she said, "Daniel asked you to tell me he was leaving. Very well you have told me. You don't need to fill the air with false compliments or try to assure me I am still capable of attracting another man." She turned to leave.

"Molly."

She did not look back even though she heard the quick urgency in his command.

He caught hold of her arm and spun her back to face him. He brought his other hand up to her upper arm and held her so she could not break free. "I was not giving you false compliments, Molly."

"Pray let me go," she said haughtily.

Proper breeding dictated that he obey her, yet he continued to hold her in a tight grasp. In fact, his grip tightened around her slender arms.

"Listen to me, Molly," he snapped.

"It does not appear I have a choice."

"No, you do not. Just because Daniel changed his mind does not mean another man might not want you. Someone else might want you even more."

"Am I to be comforted by such assurances from a man who did not even welcome me and my uncle into his house?" Molly inquired acidly.

"People can change their minds."

"Yes. Daniel has proven that. If you fear I may do something foolish because I am distraught about Daniel, you need not be concerned. I am going to go back to my room and tear up his miniature and perhaps his letters, and then I shall be perfectly fine."

The earl dropped his hands from her arms and stepped slowly back. "I am not talking about Daniel." His words were thick and husky.

Molly stood motionless. What did he mean?

"I have changed my mind about you, Molly. I see you differently than I did when you first came."

"I—I don't understand."

"I think you do, Molly."

She looked up into the burning gray eyes and saw the look of steady intent on his face. Then he put his arms around her and pulled her against him. She might have meant to protest when she lifted her face, but she found her lips caught by his.

His mouth was warm and full of purpose as she was engulfed in the wave of his embrace. For an instant she thought about pushing away. Instead, she leaned in closer. She kissed him with all the feeling she should have had only for Daniel, and she savored the sensations when his hands flexed on her back.

Each kiss is different—defined by tenderness or passion or quiet need. This kiss was full of heat and urgency, yet floating beneath the surface she sensed a calming aura of caring or perhaps of something deeper. It was hard for her to sort it all out in her mind while her body was pressed tightly against his. It was hard to sort it out when she tingled all over and when naked yearning uncurled from a long, deep sleep and crept throughout her limbs.

All kisses were meant to end. When this one did, he set her on her feet. For a moment, she was off balance, and he kept his hands on her arms to steady her. Dazed, she stared up into his eyes. Only minutes ago, she had learned she was not going to marry Daniel, and now she was standing in the earl's study kissing him. Surely this was not Lord Lindworth's way of offering comfort or even reassurance. Yet what else could it be? Unless, that is, he felt something deeper for her.

Molly put her hands up to her temples. It was too confusing. "This is the second time you have kissed me."

"Yes."

"I have not been imbibing wine this time, so my head ought to be clear. But it is not. It is swirling with a thousand thoughts." Her body still trembled from the embrace. What did this mean? Then she thought of the kindness he had shown by continuing to keep a discarded mistress in funds and asked him, "Are you doing this because you feel sorry for me?"

"No, Molly. I kissed you because I could not stop myself."

She raised a hand to keep him from saying anything else. "I need to go to my room and sort all this out. Everything is happening so suddenly."

"You are right, Molly." He sounded regretful. "It was too soon for me to act. I should have given you time. I shall ring for your maid to escort you back."

This time Molly did not object.

Chapter 11

Antonia was in her room when Molly reached it after leaving the earl. Molly wondered if her expression betrayed her confusion or if her cheeks were still flushed from the kiss.

Molly need not have worried. Her cousin's thoughts were on other matters entirely. "Henry thinks the gypsy will come tonight. Henry's friend Giles Glancy from Dover will spend the night here to help capture William Jersey. Edgar, Henry's friend from the village, is also here. Can you imagine the look on the earl's face when he discovers what we have done?"

Although Molly tried to imagine his look of surprise, the expression that came to mind was the steady, almost soft, way he had looked at her after he kissed her. Antonia had read romantic passages from novels aloud to her, but Molly had never thought to feel as captivated and lost in romance as those heroines had.

"The earl will be so proud of Henry."

Molly did not care a whit right now how he felt toward Henry. It was how he felt toward her that mattered. Or did it? She was only loosely connected to Irish nobility, she reminded herself. Yet Lord Lindworth's place in society meant everything to him. It was true he had kissed her, but he had undoubtedly kissed other women before her. He would probably kiss others after she was gone. Stealing a few kisses was one thing, but marriage was quite another.

"They have left the book in the library," Antonia confided.

Molly barely heard. The earl had said his actions were not prompted by Daniel's defection. Was that true? She could not fathom Lord Lindworth propelling her into his arms out of charity and a desire to comfort. The proper, well-bred earl would not have swept her into his arms under any circumstances. Yet he had.

"Henry left a downstairs window unlatched."

"Mmmm." Lord Lindworth said he had changed. He must have changed a great deal to draw her into his arms like that. He had, she reminded herself, kissed her once before. But that had been a chaste kiss, and although she had wondered why he had done it, she had not put overmuch weight on it. Today's kiss was far different. It was impossible not to put weight on it.

"I am going to dress myself as the maid Letty and open the window for him," Antonia said.

Molly blinked and brought her wandering thoughts to focus on her cousin's words. "Open the window for whom?"

"The gypsy." Antonia frowned. "You have not been attending. We are going to capture him tonight, and I am going to help."

Molly landed firmly back in the present. Her cousin was not going to stand unprotected near a man who might be capable of anything. What did anyone know about this gypsy besides the fact he was a thief? He might be a murderer as well.

"No, you are not, my girl," Molly said.

Antonia tossed her head in defiance. "Yes, I am. I have to. I have already told Henry I will help him."

"Then I shall tell him the plans have changed."

Antonia's lips pursed into a pout that soon became a tremble. "W—Why can't I?"

It was the question every thirteen-year-old child who ever lived had asked of every adult, Molly supposed. She softened her words. " 'Tis too dangerous. Something might go awry and you might be harmed."

"I will be careful. I promise."

Molly shook her head and led her cousin to the bed. She pushed her gently down on the side of the bed and sat down next to her. "Your father would never allow this. Since he is ill"—or pretending to be—"I must make judgments for him. I cannot allow you to put yourself in danger."

"I'm only going to open the window. The room will be dark, and he will not be able to see that I am not who I say I am."

"Antonia—"

Tears flowed down her cheeks. "I only have to lead him a few steps down to the library. Then Henry and Giles and Edgar will take charge. What can go wrong?"

"I can think of a dozen things. The gypsy might ask you a question, and the moment you open your mouth, he will realize you are Irish."

"I shall pretend I did not hear the question. I must do this or all the plans are for nothing."

"Why can't Henry capture him on the grounds

outside or even once he steps through the window?" Molly asked reasonably. "Why must it be in the library?"

"He could get away if he were still outside. The library has only one door into it, and when it is closed, he is trapped. He's devilish slippery, Molly."

That much she believed. Still, this was no task for a girl, and she was surprised Henry had embroiled Antonia. With a shake of her head, Molly said, "You are not helping, and there's an end to it."

Antonia glared at her.

"I am sorry." Molly took her hand and walked her down the hall to her room. Then she locked the door, pocketed the key, and went in search of Henry to tell him the plans had changed.

Lord Lindworth stood on the balcony outside the drawing room and finished his cheroot. It smelled strong and pungent, but his thoughts were on the delicate fragrance of Molly's hair.

"Best damned port we've ever had," Henry declared.

The earl turned to look at him. Henry had had more port than was good for him already. His words were slightly slurred, and he was talking more than usual. He was also inordinately cheerful.

"Henry, I hope you will be sober when the prince arrives tomorrow."

"Of course I will be. Plenty of time between now and tomorrow," he added.

Lord Lindworth didn't bother to reply. He turned back to look out over the garden and put his hands on the cool balustrade that ran around the balcony. The coarse grains of the stone rubbed at his palms, but he did not mind. He was thinking about Molly. What was he going to do about her?

"I have a feeling something important will happen tonight," Henry said.

Something important already had happened. Lawrence had kissed Molly Mills, and she had responded. He had felt her lithe frame press against him, and he had thought of more intimate and inappropriate things that he would like to do with her.

"Do you ever have those sorts of feelings?" Henry prompted. "You know, when you are certain something exciting is about to happen?"

"I cannot say that I have," Lawrence said briskly. "But I do have the feeling you have had as many spirits as you can hold."

Henry laughed as if his brother had just made the most delightful jest.

Lawrence bit back a scathing setdown. Had he been this foolish when he was that age?

As if Henry had read his thoughts, he said, "I know you think me a buffoon, but I warrant you'll soon change your mind. Oh, I'll own I've made a mistake or two. I know now how unwise it was to leave William Jersey in charge of the estate."

The earl held his tongue.

Henry drained the dregs from his glass. "I learned my lesson from that. It's made me a deal wiser, if you take my meaning."

"I don't take your meaning, Henry, but I see you are deep in your cups. Why don't I summon your valet and have him assist you in retiring for the night?"

"Retiring! The night has just begun."

Lawrence sighed.

A movement caught his eye, and he looked up to see Molly standing framed in the doorway. The light from the drawing room made her hair gleam a golden red. Her dress was a pale drape that made a soft silhouette around her small frame. Her face was partially shadowed by the half-light on the balcony, but he saw that her mouth was set in a tight line.

Lawrence wondered if she had come here to publicly announce that he had kissed her and to demand an accounting from him. He hoped that was not the case. He had acted rashly but from the heart. He wanted any conversation about those passionate moments to be held in private between them.

And he did intend to speak with her. This was not some passing fancy. When he was seventeen, he was in love with a wholly unsuitable woman. He remembered the relentless yearning and the way he caught his breath at the sight of her. It had been a boyish infatuation that had faded quickly. The passion and fervor he felt now gave no hint of fading.

He looked squarely into the face of what he was contemplating. Molly was neither titled nor English nor biddable. She was, however, generous with her cousin, kind to Henry, and possessed of a true heart. Was that not more important than all the trappings he had always thought so necessary? Were his feelings for her not more important than any obstacle?

"I am sorry for interrupting," she said.

Both men turned to her.

She looked at the earl. It was difficult to see into her eyes or know what she was feeling. He felt a softness toward her. And, yes, the desire to kiss her again.

"I wish to have a word alone with your brother, milord."

It was not what Lawrence had expected her to say. What business could she have with Henry that caused her to seek them out on the balcony this late at night? "Is anything wrong?" Lawrence asked quickly.

She turned away from him, as if it were somehow painful to look at him too long. "No, nothing is wrong. I only wanted to inquire of him about a book in the library."

The earl saw Henry look up sharply. "Is there a problem with the book?"

Molly glanced back toward the earl. "Not precisely."

Henry had been an indifferent schoolboy and had never been a scholar. He had not been in the library above a dozen times in the past two years. Lawrence did not believe they were talking about a book.

"Please, could we speak in private?" Molly asked.

Henry nodded and hurried out of the room after her.

Lawrence watched them go. Whatever was afoot had Henry's attention. Lawrence would like to know what they were about, but he could scarcely object to two adults speaking in private. Perhaps it had something to do with Antonia. He sensed, though, that it did not.

It had been a day of events and emotions, Lawrence reflected. Tomorrow, with the arrival of the prince, was going to be even more eventful. He wished he were looking forward to the visit with more enthusiasm. His plans were all in readiness to show the prince, neatly laid out and awaiting inspection. He should be excited. He was not.

"Lord Lindworth, forgive me for intruding."

He pivoted and blinked in surprise to see Sir Brace standing in the doorway.

"Did I startle you?"

"I am surprised to see you," the earl said truthfully. "Are you better?" he inquired politely.

"Yes." The baronet shifted uncomfortably and then walked the short distance to stand beside the earl at the balustrade. "I shall be leaving tomorrow."

Lawrence should have considered his mother's joy and his own relief. Instead, he demanded, "With your niece and daughter as well?"

"Yes. They will go, too." Sir Brace put his elbows on the rough stone and stared out into the darkness. Overhead a slip of moon shed little light, but the stars danced brightly. "My gout has improved, and Molly is most anxious to leave."

"She is?" Lawrence asked without inflection.

"Yes. I have promised her we will go. You see—" He stopped and spread his hands in a hopeless gesture. "No, I don't think you do see. You have probably never wanted something so badly you would do anything to obtain it."

The earl looked up at the stars and felt the enormous distance separating him from them. The baronet was almost right. Until recently, there had been nothing Lawrence desired that he could not obtain. Money and position had gained him entrée into the best houses. They had paved his way into the right clubs. They had made it possible for him to meet the right young women as potential marriage partners.

Money, however, could not purchase the affections of another, especially if that woman was strong-willed and independent.

Sir Brace straightened and looked at the earl. "I have taken advantage of your hospitality. I came here hoping to see the prince. I prayed for just five minutes alone with him to explain how it happened between his father and myself. I wanted a chance to apologize. I wanted to make things right so that Antonia could have the opportunities that are her birthright."

Lord Lindworth looked into the other man's eyes and saw the stark honesty. He had formed no real opinion of Sir Brace beyond the fact he was an inconvenience. Now he saw the white-haired baronet as a man for the first time. How old could Sir Brace have been when he struck the king? Twenty? A year or two older? Who among Lawrence's friends had not committed some youthful folly? Henry had allowed their whole household to be carried away. Was he to be punished for that his whole life long?

"I understand," the earl said softly.

"Only a few minutes with the prince," Sir Brace repeated.

"You will have them. I shall see to it." Lawrence fancied he had some small influence over the prince. He would have a word with the Prince Regent himself. He thought he would be inclined to be charitable.

The baronet looked at him in disbelief. Then he nodded in gratitude. "We shall go away after that and not invade your estate again."

"You will leave tomorrow?" the earl asked thickly.

"You have my word on it." Sir Brace left, walking slowly back into the drawing room.

Did Molly wish to go? Yes, of course she did. Her uncle had said so. Certainly when Lawrence had seen her only a few minutes ago, there had been nothing in her bearing to suggest kindness toward him, or even friendship.

Yet her kiss had suggested something quite different.

Molly stood across from Henry in the library and shook her head again. "I cannot allow her to put herself in danger."

Distraught, he pushed splayed fingers through his black hair and circled the room feverishly. "This is the end of all our plans." He stopped and gazed at her in reproach.

"Henry, I am sorry for that, but it cannot be helped."

"Of course it can." He became cajoling, turning eyes amazingly like his brother's on her. "I ask only this one thing. It may be the one good opportunity I ever have to make Lawrence realize I am not a complete fool. Won't you help me undertake to prove that?"

She sighed. She realized how important it was to Henry to prove himself to his older brother. "You are not making this easy for me."

- "Please reconsider."

"I cannot allow Antonia to take part." She glanced down at her own simple muslin gown and slender figure. She was taller than Antonia, it was true, but in the shadows, her height might be concealed. She wanted to help Henry. Besides, the spirit of adventure tugged at her. "However, I am willing to undertake her role."

His eyes widened with hope. "You would?"

"Yes." She owed him that much. He had been kind to her cousin in teaching her archery, and he had been pleasant to Molly throughout her visit.

"Splendid."

She basked in the beam of his smile before becoming serious. "Tell me what I am to do."

"Be in the picture gallery standing by the window shortly before midnight. William Jersey is to come to the window and knock, and you admit him. It's really quite simple."

"What if he asks me a question?"

"Put your finger to your lips to signal that he must not talk."

She nodded.

"Then you have only to lead him to the library. Giles and Edgar and I will take matters from there." He grinned at her. "You're a right one, Molly, to help me."

She gave him a small answering smile and started back to her room. She did not enlighten Henry that she was doing this for other reasons besides helping him. One was that having something to do took her mind off Henry's brother, and she very much wished to push him from her mind.

As she moved through the halls, she reflected that she should be grieving for the loss of Daniel. Yet Daniel was the furthest thing from her mind. He had been replaced in her affections by a man who not only was unsuited to her temperament but who would never deign to consider her for anything beyond stolen kisses.

Would he?

The earl was a man of honor, Molly knew. After the first kiss, he had come back to her to apologize. After this most recent, far more torrid kiss, would he again apologize? She wondered what she would say if he did.

As she strolled past the pictures of Lindworth ancestors, she knew she was not sorry for the kiss. It had opened up doors inside herself she had only suspected were there. His kiss had also generated sadness, because it hurt to know that she was capable of such feeling and to know she would be denied those feelings the rest of her life.

Perhaps with another man, she consoled herself as she rounded a corner and moved toward her door.

The sadness arched back at her, contradicting her and telling her she would never feel this way with another man.

Molly stopped with her hand on the doorknob. She was not some simpering little miss who was going to fade quietly away and disappear to Ireland forever. She had more pluck than that. She would tell Lord Lindworth—Lawrence—that she had been moved by his kisses. She would demand that he tell her what his true feelings were for her. Whatever the answer, at least she would know.

Molly did not care a fig that it would break every rule of English breeding to make such a bold statement. Hang the English, and the Irish with them. She was not going to him as a country; she was going to him as a woman. She would demand his answer as a man.

Molly started down the hall in search of the earl. She found him still standing on the balcony.

"Oh, I thought you might be Henry," he said impassively.

"No. I do not know where he went."

"Probably into town on some fool's errand," he said irritably.

His words pulled her away from what she had been about to say. "Henry worships you, you know."

At his surprised look, she continued, "I know he has acted impetuously at times, but he longs for your approval."

The night air was chilly around them, and the lights from the drawing room did little to light the balcony. As Molly stood facing the earl, she felt a wealth of unspoken emotions and confusion. They should have been discussing their own feelings for each other, but it was important to her to intercede on Henry's behalf in what little way she could.

Even in the faint light, she could see that Lawrence was staring at her in amazement. Somewhere in the distance, a clock chimed.

Suddenly she realized it was getting late. She still had to find clothes to wear for her part as the maid Letty, and she had to get dressed and back downstairs.

Tomorrow she would speak to the earl and tell him the real reason she had sought him out.

"I must go. Think upon what I said about Henry." She hurried away.

The house lay sunk in a deep silence. Outside, clouds drifted across the moon. Molly stood by the window in the gallery in the dark room, cloaked in a black gown and with her hair tumbling forward to partially hide her face.

Now and again she looked out the window. Every

tree seemed a man's shadow. Every bush moving in the wind looked like a person stealing forward.

Molly knew Henry and the two others were just down the hall. Now that she was here, though, enveloped in darkness and waiting with tensed muscles, the library seemed a very long distance away. What if the gypsy came and she could not coax him to the library? What if he recognized that she was not Letty, and Henry did not hear her cries?

She was being fanciful, Molly chided herself. Her imagination would have done one of Antonia's gothic heroines proud. Molly was a mature woman, and she could handle whatever situation arose.

What was that noise?

She listened with every frozen inch of her body. When she peered out into the darkness, she saw nothing. Henry had been certain the gypsy would come tonight. What if he was wrong?

Then she saw it. A figure—large and dark and ominous—stalked toward the house. She beat back the impulse to flee. She could not do anything so cowardly. Her task was quite simple. She had only to stand here and let the man in.

The figure drew closer. She read menace in every line of his frame as he crept with stealth and purpose. He stopped outside the window. She had not known he would look so large or threatening.

Her hands shook as she reached over and pushed the window open.

He stepped in.

Her nerve almost deserted her. He might have a knife or even a gun. Strengthening her resolve, she put her hand out to take his.

He fitted his gloved hand into hers and followed her into the dark cave of the house. Away from the window, they had not even the faint light of the moon to guide them. Molly had not realized it would be this dark. She was not even sure she could find the library.

"Where is it?" he whispered.

She put her fingers to her lips, then realized he could not see her gesture. "Shhh."

"No one can hear us. The family sleeps abovestairs."

"Shhh."

"Letty?"

"Shhh." She felt his hand tighten on hers, and he pulled her to a stop. Should she scream for Henry?

"Where are you leading me?" he hissed. His breath was harsh and full of garlic on her face.

"To the library," she managed to say. The tremor in her voice helped block some of her accent.

It scarcely mattered, anyway. Suddenly someone was running down the hall toward them holding a candle aloft.

"What the devil?" He let go of Molly.

"Antonia!" Molly screamed just as the child came to a terrified stop only a few feet from them.

The man whirled to look at Molly. "You ain't Letty."

Molly looked wildly around and began screaming for help. Within moments she heard the sound of thundering footsteps. It must be Henry and his companions, she thought with relief. Somehow the candle was extinguished and she found herself shrinking away from the noise of muffled thuds and groans. All the while, she groped the air, searching desperately for Antonia's hand. People brushed past her and fell against her, and Molly found herself dodging around crazily in the darkness. She had to find Antonia. The first two hands she grasped were large ones with hair on the back. She hurled them away.

"Antonia! Where are you?"

Someone grabbed her by the wrist. It was a large hand, and she bit into it.

"Molly!" She stopped short of a second bite. She recognized that voice as the earl's.

Then there was light. Startled servants in nightwear appeared bearing wavering candles. Molly had a hazy vision of Uncle Brace standing with the others. She saw Antonia peering down at a man who lay on the floor. Henry still struggled with another man Molly had never seen before.

"Henry, let him go," Lawrence shouted.

"He's a thief." Henry took another swing and missed.

"Let him go. He's Mr. Miller."

Where had she heard that name before?

Henry's hand fell to his side. "The man you hired to find the gypsy?"

"Yes."

Mr. Miller jerked out of Henry's grasp and dragged himself to his feet. A large bruise was already beginning to swell around his right eye.

"Sorry," Henry mumbled, and clapped him on the shoulder. "Didn't mean to do you an injury. Well, I did mean to, but that was before I realized who you were. No harm done."

"Please do not touch me again," Mr. Miller said stiffly.

Molly looked back up at the earl, who still held her hand. His hair was disheveled, indicating he, too, had been caught in the fight. A cut grazed his cheek. He had never looked more handsome to her.

The gypsy lying on the ground moaned.

"I caught him," Henry announced proudly, and went to stand over him. "Move away, Antonia. This could be a trick. He might spring back to life."

Antonia came to stand beside her, and Molly bent to kiss her cousin's cheek. It would be pointless to scold her for leaving the room. Later she would find out how Antonia had effected that. No doubt the girl had climbed out a window, Molly reasoned. At any rate, if she had been in Antonia's shoes, she probably would have done the same thing.

She was not in Antonia's shoes, though. She was in her own little kid boots, and the earl still held her hand. She did not let go.

"What in the devil is going on here?" Lawrence demanded of Henry.

Molly pressed his hand hard in warning.

"Henry, are you responsible for making such a mull of everything? Don't you realize that I had hired a man to—"

This time she squeezed his hand so hard that she felt him stiffen. He looked down at her. She saw the light of understanding come on, as if he recalled their discussion on the balcony about Henry.

"I caught him, Lawrence," Henry said. "I caught William Jersey."

"I was right after the gypsy," Mr. Miller interjected sourly. "It was not necessary to lead such a merry chase. I had him well in hand."

Lawrence ignored Mr. Miller and turned to his brother. Henry stood uncertainly, his gaze fixed on Lawrence.

"You caught him, Henry," he said. Slowly a grin

crept over his face. "So you did, Henry. Damned fine work. Damned fine."

Henry blinked.

"I'm proud of you."

Henry shrugged with excessive modesty, as if it had been the merest trifle.

"Had him in hand," Mr. Miller muttered.

Henry stood beaming with satisfaction, then announced, "Giles and I shall ride for the constable."

The earl stepped forward to congratulate Giles and Edgar. Mr. Miller stood complaining in the center of the room. The gypsy still lay supine on the elegant polished oak floors.

"Giles, you and Edgar keep an eye on the fellow. Antonia, to bed with you." Lord Lindworth took a taper from a servant and tugged at Molly's hand. "Miss Mills, I'd like a word with you."

She followed him mutely down the hall to a large room illuminated only by the flickering light from the taper.

"That was kind of you to praise Henry," she said. "It has made him feel grand."

He closed the door behind him, put the candle on the mantel, and turned to face her. He looked at her grimly. "What was your part in this, Molly?"

"Why, only to let William Jersey in the window."

"A wise action." His words dripped sarcasm. "He is only the size of a baited bear and probably just as dangerous. Don't you realize you could have been hurt?"

"Pray do not shout at me."

"How do you think I felt when I heard you screaming? It was like a cold knife going through me."

"Oh," she said in a small voice. She had been

202

ready to do battle, but his words changed that. He was shouting because he had been that worried about her.

She gazed up into eyes as full of emotion as any she had ever seen. She wondered how she had failed to read in those gray depths what was so clearly written now. He reached out to touch her hair, and she was suddenly breathless.

His fingers moved down to stroke her cheek. "Molly, you must stop being so beautiful, or I will continue to lure you into dark closets and kiss you."

She was glad when he stopped talking and bent to kiss her. It started like the heat from the tip of a candle, warm and smooth and reassuring. But she was quickly drawn down into the hottest part of the flame. She felt the scorching intensity of his passion, and she felt her own desire reaching out to meet his.

Each kiss was deeper than the one before. Each more searching, more fulfilling, and each opened further doors of wonder. She clung to him as tightly as if she would burn to cinders without him.

When he finally put her away from him, they were both flushed.

"I don't mind you kissing me," she whispered.

He chuckled low in his throat. "This is why young ladies should always have chaperons."

"You and your rules," she mumbled into his cravat.

They lapsed back into a flurry of kisses. Now and again he murmured something against her cheek or blew kisses into her ear. She was losing her thoughts altogether when he said, "I don't want you to leave Wicklowe Hall. Ever."

Flushed and disheveled, she emerged from his embrace. "Are you asking me to marry you?"

"I must speak with your uncle first. These things must be done properly."

"Of course," she murmured, and started to kiss him again. She drew back, struck by another thought. "What will your mother say?"

"That you can be made to give a good accounting of yourself with the proper training. She will be glad to undertake that." He shook her gently. "Molly, you needn't fear I intend to try to make you a pattern card of respectability. I know you will always follow your own mind."

"And you still want me?"

"Yes. Because you will also follow your own heart, and you have taught me to follow mine."

She smiled at him. "I will follow my heart. It has led me to you, and I do not think I could do better than that."

They had a lot to say to each other, but they had all the years ahead of them in which to say them. It was more important now to bury herself in his embrace and feel the warmth of his love flow over her.